Adrift

JULIE BURTINSHAW

RAINCOAST BOOKS

Vancouver

Raincoast Books acknowledges the ongoing financial support of the Government of Canada through The Canada Council for the Arts and the Book Publishing Industry Development Program (BPIDP); and the Government of British Columbia through the BC Arts Council.

Edited by Elizabeth McLean
Text design by Ingrid Paulson
Map on page six by Peter Moffat.

NATIONAL LIBRARY OF CANADA CATALOGUING IN PUBLICATION DATA
Burtinshaw, Julie, 1958–
    Adrift

ISBN 1-55192-469-2

    I. Title.
PS8553.U69623A73 2002   jC813'.6   C2001-911679-9
PZ7.B947A73 2002

Library of Congress Catalogue Number: 2002102365

Raincoast Books   In the United States:
9050 Shaughnessy Street   Publishers Group West
Vancouver, British Columbia   1700 Fourth Street
Canada   v6p 6e5   Berkeley, California
www.raincoast.com   94710

Printed in Canada by Webcom

1 2 3 4 5 6 7 8 9 10

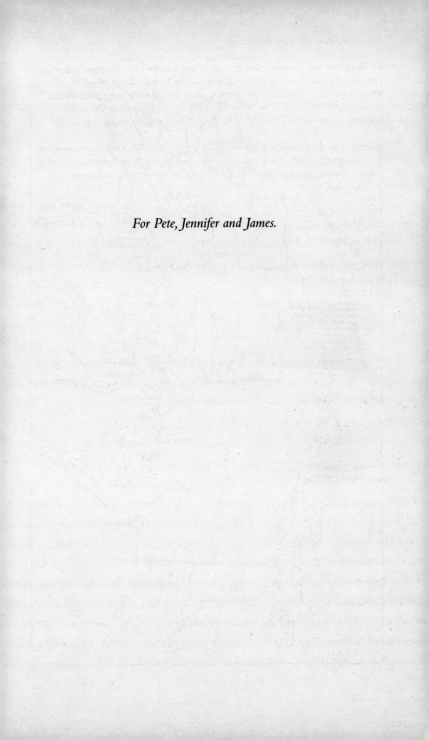

For Pete, Jennifer and James.

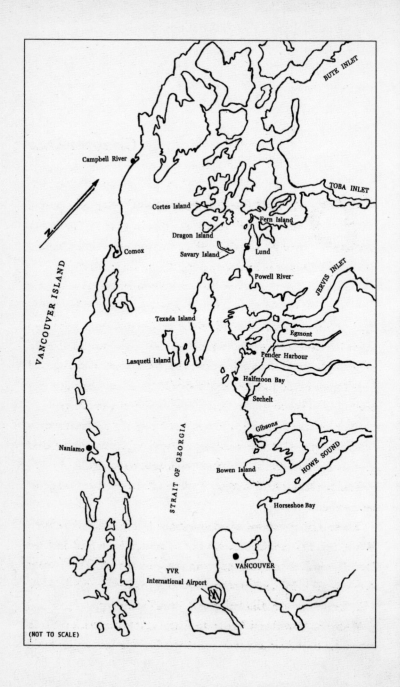

BUTE INLET

Campbell River

TOBA INLET

Cortes Island

Fern Island

Dragon Island

Lund

Comox

Savary Island

Powell River

JERVIS INLET

VANCOUVER ISLAND

Texada Island

Egmont

Pender Harbour

Lasqueti Island

Halfmoon Bay

Sechelt

Gibsons

Naniamo

HOWE SOUND

STRAIT OF GEORGIA

Bowen Island

Horseshoe Bay

VANCOUVER

YVR
International Airport

(NOT TO SCALE)

Chapter One

"**D**AVID!**"** Barely audible. "David." His mother raised her voice just enough so that he could pick out her words. "Could I talk to you for a moment, please?" David hesitated before answering, then: "Sure, Mum."

He glanced nervously at his best friend Bill, settled on the ground a few metres to his right, before he refocused his attention on his mother. She stood on the back porch, her hand up to shade her eyes from the hazy June sunshine. She was still dressed in her nightgown and the long hair that she'd once been so proud of fell uncombed past her slight shoulders. Even from this distance, David could see the dark circles under her tired eyes.

"I'm coming," he called to her. "You go back inside. Just give me five minutes." When she'd gone, David unconsciously relaxed his fists and allowed his breathing to return to normal.

The last thing he'd wanted was for Bill to see the change in his mother.

There'd be questions asked, questions David couldn't answer. Worse yet, Bill might pretend not to notice how frail and sad David's mother had become over the past winter. That's what everyone else did, and in some ways that made this whole thing a lot harder to bear. But Bill hadn't even looked up.

Relieved, David crawled on his knees across the brick patio to where his friend crouched in concentration. On his way, he lifted the occasional brick to scoop up a fleeing wood bug in his strong fist. When he touched the prehistoric-looking insects, their corrugated grey bodies folded into hard silver balls, and he thought of knights and armour and chain mail vests. He rolled each insect gently in his fingers before dropping it into the roomy pocket of his cargo pants. He and Bill collected the bugs to feed to the furry wolf spider that lived under the riser on the second step. David was not a cruel boy, far from it. He fed her because he suspected she was alone and he found her beautiful in a remote, unworldly way.

"I gotta go." David stood up abruptly, afraid that his mother might reappear on the back porch any second.

"I know. Me, too." Bill emptied his pockets in front of the spider's hole. "Bon appétit," he said in her general direction, and to David, "Do you want to come over to my house for dinner tonight? Mum always makes way too much food, and I think she kind of misses you, since you've made yourself so scarce."

"Some other time," replied David. "But thanks."

"He can't," called Laura.

David had forgotten all about his little sister. She'd kept her distance for a change, probably because she despised any sort of bug. Laura was three years younger than David, a fifth-grader.

Last month, David had unearthed his old ant farm out of the pile of once-treasured toys discarded in the basement. Perhaps, he'd reasoned, if she had her own ant colony to care for, Laura might finally understand his fascination with insects and biology. Instead, she'd watched the ants with detached interest and forgotten to water the colony. Within a week, they were dead.

Even a harmless worm could elicit a screech of disgust from her that echoed through their neighbourhood. David's hobby as a backyard scientist often depended on a good field assistant. His little sister was hopeless.

"He can't," she repeated to Bill. "He has to cook. Mum doesn't cook anymore."

"Shut up, Laura." David glared at her. He'd warned her not to say a word about their personal business, not even to best friends: *"What goes on in this house stays in this house,"* he'd said.

Bill raised his eyebrows and David shot him a warning look. "Not tonight," he snapped.

"Whatever," Bill said. "I thought I'd ask anyway. Maybe some other time. I'll see you at school tomorrow," he added tentatively.

David shrugged. "I guess," he said, "and thanks for the invite."

"No problem." Bill grabbed his bike and disappeared through the back gate. David watched him go, unable to shake the thought that, as usual, he'd handled everything wrong.

"Look at me!" Laura had tucked Susie, the doll that never left her side, safely into her shirt and scrambled up to the top of the huge old maple tree that grew at the foot of their long narrow garden. "Come on up!" she urged her brother.

"I can't. Mum needs me." David reached into his pocket and extracted the wood bugs he'd collected. He placed their armoured bodies in front of the black hole where the wolf spider lived. He lined them up like targets in a video game, then he took the back stairs two at a time. It had always been this way between him and Laura. In spite of her aversion to anything creepy-crawly, she was the risk-taker and he was the sensible one. More and more often, David wished things were the other way around.

He paused before he entered the house. Behind him, the afternoon dissolved into evening as the sun sank gradually behind Lake Ontario, the ocean-size lake that lay only two blocks from where they'd always lived, on Toronto's eclectic west side. The shadow of their tall Victorian house stretched lazily across the overgrown lawn. David shivered, although the heavy, warm air promised a hot summer.

Their house sat shrouded in dusky silence. David willed the lights on, but nothing happened. Nothing moved. No curtains fluttered, no delicious dinner smells filled the kitchen and drifted out the back door the way they once had. Nothing was the way it had been.

"Mum?" David pushed open the back door. He saw the silhouette of his mother at the far end of the kitchen. "Mum. You wanted to talk to me?" He spoke softly, the way he would to a frightened child. "Why don't we turn on the lights?"

"Yes. It totally slipped my mind." Yet she stayed in the shadows, so David hit the switch. The lights illuminated her haggard features and she retreated farther back into the corner. "Light gives me a headache."

"Mum." He began to feel a familiar exasperation building. "What did you want to talk to me about? Are you feeling okay? Better?" he said hopefully.

Laura entered the kitchen behind him. "Hi, Mum." She slipped out of her runners and made a beeline for the fridge.

"Hi, honey." Her mother smiled weakly. "Are you hungry? What about you, David?"

"It's dinnertime. Most kids are hungry at dinner," David said shortly.

She dropped her eyes, and for the second time in ten minutes, a sense of guilt threatened to overwhelm David. He couldn't do or say anything right anymore! He swallowed quickly as a large tear rolled down his mother's thin cheek. When she spoke, he avoided her eyes. "I know. I'm so sorry. I can't help it. The doctors …"

David reached over, intending to give her a hug, but instead he gripped her shoulders firmly and pointed her in the direction of the stairs. "It's okay, Mum. I know what the doctors say. What did you want to talk to me about?"

"Um. Dinner. I thought I might get up, but … I don't know why I'm so tired all the time." She started slowly up the narrow stairs.

Like a seasoned actor, David masked the anger he felt with false enthusiasm. "Why don't you go up and lie down on your bed? Laura and I will take care of us. I'm a great cook!"

"No, you're not," Laura said. "You only know how to cook two things, and I'm tired of both of them."

"I'll order a pizza. Pepperoni and cheese."

"I'm sick of pizza," Laura whined. "We have pizza all the time."

David sighed. Nobody could afford to eat pizza all the time. Some kids might think ordering pizza a couple of times a week was a treat, but in truth, David agreed with her.

"I'm sick of pizza too," he said. "We could make something."

"Like what?" Laura wanted to know.

"I don't know. Peanut butter sandwiches or Kraft Dinner, or a ham and cheese sandwich."

That was about the extent of David's menu range and they both knew it.

"Why doesn't Mum cook anymore?" Laura followed her mother's disappearing legs with her eyes. "I want something good, like roast chicken, and mashed potatoes with gravy. I miss the old food."

Ten minutes later, David stabbed the knife handle into the

peanut butter jar. He licked his sticky fingers and carried two thick sandwiches into the den where Laura sat hypnotized in front of their favourite show, *The Simpsons*.

"Dinner." He dropped the messy sandwiches onto the coffee table and sank down in the sofa beside his sister. At half-past eight, Laura got up and turned on the lights. "This house is always so dark," she complained.

A few minutes later, they heard the soft footsteps of their mother coming down the hall. She'd made an effort to fix herself up a bit, and for a second she was the mother she'd been before the sadness had begun to steal her away. She'd tied her hair back in a neat ponytail, washed her face and dressed in a knee-length yellow skirt and blue blouse.

"I see you've taken care of dinner," she said, smiling.

David smiled back, a genuine smile. "I left the peanut butter and jam out if you want a sandwich," he said. "Or you might want ham and cheese."

"You know, I just might," his mother replied. "I love ham and cheese with plenty of mayonnaise and mustard."

"Try eating it every night," Laura mumbled.

"Perhaps," their mother suggested, "tomorrow night we could do something together, the three of us. Maybe we could go out for dinner."

"Okay," agreed Laura. "And tonight you could tuck me and Susie in and read us a story."

"Of course I will." She gently stroked Laura's sandy yellow hair, then touched Susie's plastic arm affectionately. "Tomorrow we'll have some fun."

David stood up, clicked off the television and brushed past his mother and sister. "You can't read to a doll," he muttered.

"Hey," Laura squealed. "Turn it back on. You're not the king of TV."

"I've got homework," he said, tossing the clicker to Laura. "By the way, Mum, tomorrow is Friday."

His mother turned her distracted gaze on him. "Is something wrong, dear?"

"Tomorrow," he repeated patiently, "is Friday. Tomorrow we go to Dad's."

"Oh. Of course." She wrung her hands together. "It slipped my mind. Well, maybe your father would like to go out for dinner with us. It would be just like old times."

"We're going to the cottage. Besides, I don't really think Dad would want to." David saw he'd hurt her. He saw it in her slumping shoulders and pained expression. Well, too bad. He hurt, too. He brushed his guilt aside. "I'll be in my room. Good night."

They'd been planning the trip to the cottage for weeks. Every year, on the Victoria Day weekend, for as long as David could remember, his family would pile into their car and head north on Highway 11 to Muskoka to open their cottage for the summer. This year, not only were they two weeks late, but only three of them would be going.

Last Thanksgiving, when they'd closed the Pine Lake cottage for the winter, David hadn't realized that that trip would be the last one they'd make as a family. Six weeks later, on November 27, saying he couldn't take it anymore, Dad had moved out, and now almost seven months had gone by. In less than two weeks, it would be the end of June and school would break for summer holidays. David would leave grade eight behind.

Last summer, like the one before and the one before that, Bill had spent two weeks with David's family at their cottage. David's

parents had finally allowed the boys to take the canoe out by themselves. Last summer, everything seemed perfect. They'd spent the
long, hot days paddling over every centimetre of the lake. Sometimes
they'd float across the water to the candy store at the south end, or
head to the north end to leap off the smoky granite cliffs. Other
days, they'd paddle out to the tiny island in the middle of the lake
to build a fort, or swim, or play cards, or lie around in the sun and
talk about girls and bikes or anything else that came to mind. They'd
return in the late afternoon to the smell of freshly baked cookies
coming from the kitchen, where David's mum would have started
dinner preparations.

He hadn't noticed any changes in his mother last August, not
big ones anyway, although looking back, he realized that the signs
had been there for a long time. Little things, like last year when
he'd found her sitting on her bed crying softly. He'd asked her
what was wrong, and she'd replied, "I don't really know. Nothing
at all, I guess." Or the days, infrequent at first, when he'd returned
home from school to find no food in the house. "I'm too tired
to go grocery shopping," she'd say, apologetically.

David had done his best to understand. He'd even shielded
Laura from his mother's increasingly unpredictable moods, and
made excuses for his father's prolonged absences from the house.
"Dad's working late, again," he'd say, or "Mum's had a bad day.
Let's go outside."

David's mother loved to garden, but in the spring of last year,
she had suddenly stopped. It wasn't so noticeable at the cottage,
where plants grew wild, but at home the neglected garden grew
tangled, weeds flourished, and Dad, who had never liked yard
work, complained bitterly about having to do all the mowing and
pruning by himself.

David knew something was really wrong when he brought his report card home last October. His marks were still good, a solid B+ average. First-rate marks would cheer them up. David's parents put a lot of store in high grades, especially when a long line of "Gs" for Good Effort accompanied those grades. He'd run all the way home through the slushy rain, ahead of Laura, and he'd found the house silent and apparently empty.

"Mum!" he yelled, not sure whether to be angry or scared. He pulled off his wet boots and chucked them in the general direction of the heater vent. "Mum!"

No answer. Above his head, the floor creaked. Relieved, David bolted up the stairs. "Mum! I've got my report card." He waved the brown envelope in the air as if it were the Stanley Cup. Good marks meant rewards, and David had his eye on a new video game.

"Mum." Her bedroom door was closed — that was odd. He knocked, and opened the door. "Mum? Are you in there? I've got my ... Mum. Are you okay? Mum?" *Adults don't cry. At least not his adults. Do they?*

She gazed at him blankly through strands of dull, dishevelled hair. "I'm not myself," she said.

"I've got my report," David whispered. He placed it on her bedside table. "I think I did really well." He backed slowly out of the room. "I'll call Dad at the office." He left his report card face up on the table. Printed in bold letters across the top was John and Elizabeth Garrett. He still didn't know, seven months later, whether either of his parents had looked at it, or even opened it.

That was the first night he'd made dinner for himself and Laura, peanut butter and banana sandwiches. What a novelty! They ate in front of the TV, and waited for their father to come home. David took a sandwich up to his mother. "Thank you, dear, but

I'm really not hungry."

"Mum has the flu," he told Laura.

At eleven o'clock they went to bed. Just after midnight, David heard the front door close softly. He crawled out of bed and went downstairs.

"Hi, David," his father sounded tired. "You're up late."

"I called you at the office. You never called back. There's something wrong with Mum."

"I know," his father replied wearily. "I know … you go up to bed. Don't worry about her. I'll be up in a minute."

David had fallen asleep curled up like a wood bug. No one mentioned report cards the next morning, nor the day after, nor the day after that. A cloak of silence hung over the house, interrupted by whispered conversations about depression, visits to psychologists, meetings with psychiatrists, and the terrible possibility of a separation between his parents.

"How come you don't go home for lunch anymore?" Bill asked David one day while they were walking home from school.

"I don't feel like it," David lied. "That's what babies do."

Bill nodded. He'd envied David's lunches at home. His parents both worked full-time, and he'd always had to eat at school. "Good," he said. "I was hoping you'd figure that out one day."

◐

The phone catapulted David back to the present. He raced down the hall and picked it up on the third ring. "Hello."

"Hi, David."

"Hi, Dad. You're not cancelling or anything, are you?"

"Of course not. I just wanted to remind you two to take all

your stuff for the weekend to school tomorrow. We'll leave as soon as you're out."

"No problem," replied David. "Dad, do you think Bill could come with us?"

"Sure. I haven't seen Bill in a while. That sounds great." He paused. "David, how's your mum?"

"She's okay tonight, I guess. She's up and dressed. She said she'd read Laura and her stupid doll a story."

"Good. I'm glad to hear it. David, there's one more thing I want to tell you."

"Sure." David knew by his father's tone that he was about to hear something he wouldn't like.

"Kathleen's coming to the cottage. I think it's time you met her in person, instead of on the phone. Getting to know her is going to be the best thing for you children," he added firmly.

Kathleen Novak: His dad's new girlfriend. Kathleen: Mum's depression wasn't her fault, but it sure didn't help matters much. Kathleen: Well, they were going to have to meet her sometime.

"Whatever," said David. "I'll see you tomorrow." He hung up and went back to his bedroom where nobody would bother him.

Chapter Two

BILL answered the phone, his voice groggy. "Hello," he mumbled.

"Wake up," said David. "School starts in twenty minutes."

Bill groaned. "I'm going to be late again. What time is it?"

"Eight-twenty. Why don't you ask your parents to wake you up before they leave for work?"

"They did, but I must have gone back to sleep."

"Oh." David didn't feel a lot of sympathy for Bill. He'd been getting himself and Laura up most mornings for the past seven months. "Do you want to come to the cottage with us this weekend?" He hadn't called Bill last night. He'd needed time to think about whether or not he wanted Bill to meet Kathleen.

"Who's us?" Bill liked details before he said yes to anything.

"Me, Laura and Laura's annoying friend Lin — you know Lin Chang — my dad and … Kathleen." It felt odd saying her name out loud.

"Kathleen? Oh. The girlfriend. Are you … I mean, does that bother you?" Bill asked.

"No. Should it … ?" Silence on the end of the phone. "Well, it does a bit, I guess," David said honestly.

"I'm in," Bill said. "I'll call my mum at her office, but she'll say yes."

"Great." David meant it. "Bring your sleeping bag and stuff to school. Dad's picking us up at three o'clock."

David hung up and dragged his backpack down the stairs. They'd had a good morning. His mother had been up first for a change. When she'd called them downstairs, cereal and toast were on the table and their lunches were made, just like old times. David's guilt about leaving her alone all weekend disappeared.

When it was time to go, Laura threw her arms around her mother. "Bye, Mum," she said, "I love you. See you Sunday night."

David gave her a quick peck on her cheek. "Are you sure you're going to be okay?" he asked.

"I'll be fine. Rose is coming over on Saturday, so I won't be alone." Rosa Fasullo, their mum's best friend, would take care of things.

"That's great. I love you, Mum." David followed Laura out the door. His mother would probably go straight back to bed, but he appreciated the effort she'd made.

Laura and David weren't to blame for her illness. Her doctor had explained everything to them. She'd said it wasn't their fault that their mother cried all the time and didn't get dressed. Depression does that to people. It was no one's fault. It was something in her brain that caused the sadness, a chemical imbalance, but sometimes David sure felt guilty. And sometimes he just felt angry.

He made it to his first class just before the final bell went. He opened his Socials book to a blank page and began to sketch a detailed picture of his red canoe.

"David!" Mrs. Johnston's raspy voice cut into his thoughts, and he looked up, startled. He hated Mrs. Johnston, also known as "The Creature." He hated the way she picked on all the kids, and he loathed the big mole that protruded from her angular chin. Six long black hairs grew out of it. Why didn't she have it removed? "You can either share your daydream with the rest of the class, or better yet, do as I've asked," she said sarcastically.

Everyone twittered. Behind him, Tom Cross nudged his leg. "You're dead," he whispered. David snapped his notebook shut and pulled himself upright. "I'm sorry, I, uh, uh, could you repeat the question?"

The class erupted in laughter, but only for a second. One glare from The Creature stopped them. She terrified all of them. Even the most obnoxious kids didn't dare disobey her.

"There was no question asked. I simply requested that you hand your homework to the person seated ahead of you. I'm sure there must be an excellent reason as to why you've failed to follow my direction. I can hardly wait to hear it."

David squirmed. The Creature waited. The class waited. "I was thinking about something else," he said. *My mother is losing her mind and I have to spend the weekend with my dad's girlfriend.* He fumbled in his backpack and finally extracted a wad of paper, which he held out to her gingerly. "Sorry. Sorry, Mrs. Johnston."

She accepted his crumpled homework gravely. "It's your parents you'll be apologizing to when they see your final marks," she said, smiling nastily. The long hairs on the mole bobbed up and down as she spoke.

There was truth in her prediction. David had always been a good student, but his marks had dropped significantly after Christmas, and if his parents bothered to open his next report card, he'd be in deep trouble. At lunch, he told Bill the story in detail, and although he laughed when he imitated The Creature, it rankled David that she was right.

The two boys ate together every noon in the cafeteria, which was really the gymnasium. It had outgrown the student population long ago and David hated the nauseating smell of tuna, hard-boiled eggs and overripe fruit that permeated the cramped, sticky space. *Only two more weeks until summer holidays,* he thought, taking a bite out of his Nutella sandwich.

"I can't wait for summer," Bill said, reading David's mind. "I hope I get to spend lots of time at your cottage again this year."

"Me, too," agreed David.

The boys spent lunch hour discussing their weekend plans, and the rest of the afternoon dreaming about the lake. At three o'clock they burst out of the school doors, where David's dad, Laura and Lin waited expectantly in the car. David jumped in beside his father. "Where's Kathleen?" he demanded.

"Hello to you, too," his father laughed.

"Hi, Mr. Garrett," said Bill. "Thanks for inviting me."

"Hello, Billy." David flushed. His father still treated them like babies. "Glad to have you. Kathleen will drive up in her own car after work." Kathleen was vice-president of a big software firm that had offices across Canada, and David and Laura had decided long ago that she practically lived at her work. "Will Rosa be staying with your mother this weekend?"

"Yup," replied Laura happily, buckling her seat belt around both her and Susie.

It infuriated David the way his father always pretended to care about their mother. If he cared, he'd never have left. He sighed audibly.

"Good," their father nodded. "Everyone settled? Excellent. We're off!"

The drive north to Muskoka took two and a half hours. The heavy Friday afternoon traffic snaked its way out of Toronto in the weekly exodus to cottage country. It was a hot, sticky day, typical of early summer, and they drove with the air conditioning on and the windows up, even though Laura insisted on opening her window every chance she got.

"I'm starved," she said after about twenty minutes. It used to be the big family joke, how Laura was always hungry as soon as they hit the 401, but this time nobody laughed.

They stopped for dinner at their favourite burger place on Highway 11, and rolled into the cottage just before six o'clock. The kids piled out of the car and dashed for the lake. "Hold on a second," protested Mr. Garrett. "Everyone has to help unload the car, then you're free for the night."

They lugged the food and bags inside. While Mr. Garrett unpacked the groceries, David, Laura, Lin and Bill claimed their rooms. "No boys allowed in our room!" shouted Laura.

"Why don't you kids get out of here? Go see if the water is warm enough for a swim," said Mr. Garrett.

Bill, Laura and Lin took off outside, but David hung back. The cottage was exactly as he'd remembered it. Family photographs covered the mantle above the stone fireplace. There were pictures of David and Laura on water skis, pictures of his mother and father sunning on the dock, pictures of all of them leaping into the lake, or sitting down to huge summer feasts in the outdoor kitchen. David picked up his favourite. In it, Mum leaned into Dad's tanned arms, an enormous smile on her face, while a much younger David and Laura peeked through their father's legs. It had been taken on the dock in early summer four years ago, when they were still a happy, normal family.

He must have sighed because his father said, "What's wrong, David? You sound like you've just lost your best friend."

"Nothing." But to himself he thought, *Everything. What an inane question!*

"You don't have to tell me. This past year has been hard on all of us."

"Why'd you leave us?" David picked up the photograph and touched his mother's face.

His father put down a jug of milk and approached David. He placed his hands on his son's shoulders, but David shook them off. "Because I couldn't stay," he said. "I tried."

"Not hard enough," replied David icily. He put the picture down and walked over to the plate-glass window that stared out to the lake. Below him, Bill, Laura and Lin sat on the dock, dangling their toes in the blue water.

"David. I wasn't going to tell you this until the end of the weekend, when I had some time with you and Laura alone, but I might as well take advantage of having you here without interruptions. Your mother hasn't been well for some time, but she's worse now. The doctor has switched her medication, and she's very positive, but your mum needs a lot of rest. I have to work …"

David didn't turn around. "What are you saying, Dad?" The small vein in David's forehead began to throb. Behind him he heard his father slump down into the old yellow armchair.

"We've hired someone, a care worker, to visit your mother once a day for the whole summer. My insurance at work will cover the cost. She'll be in intensive counselling, but like I said, she'll need plenty of rest …" He paused, but when David said nothing, continued. "David, your mother can't take care of you and Laura, not when school's out."

"Who do you think has been taking care of us while school is in?" David snapped. "You're always at work, except for weekends, and then you're so busy with What's Her Name, we hardly see you."

"That's not true, David, but I refuse to argue with you. You and your sister are going to spend the summer with Aunt Jennifer.

It's the best thing for you both. It's all arranged."

David leaned against the windowpane. All his energy seemed to drain out of his body, and he thought he might sink to the floor. Outside, the sun glinted on the water. The heat radiated off the sun-drenched glass and the warmth intensified his headache. "Aunt Jennifer? Mum's sister in British Columbia? We hardly know her!"

"Yes." Behind him, his father rose and began pacing back and forth between the kitchen and living room. "You *do* know her. We went out for Christmas when you were eight and Laura was five. She has a place on an island off the West Coast. She and Elizabeth spent their summers there as kids. She's really nice," he added lamely. "She writes cookbooks."

"Really nice," David repeated. "Well, I hope that makes you feel better, Dad. It'd be a drag to send us away to stay with someone who wasn't *really nice*. Does she have mental problems, too? I've heard it runs in families." David swung around to face his father, flushed by anger.

"David, you're not making this easy for me, but why would you? Depression can run in families, or it might just appear in individuals. I don't have all the answers. I'm sorry. I have to work and I don't know what else to do."

"No, you don't have all the answers." David's eyes narrowed. "But you have one. Get rid of the kids." He turned and began to walk out of the room, his movements slow and deliberate, but the sound of the front door squeaking open stopped him.

"Hello, John. And you must be David."

Kathleen. She stood on the stoop, one foot in the room, the other on the porch. She was taller than David's mother and wore her brown hair cropped close to her ears. Her eyes smiled. David glared at her. "I'm going outside," he said.

"Did I walk in at an awkward moment?" Kathleen held David's stare, but directed her question at his father. "I'll just get the rest of my things from the car."

David waited until she'd gone back outside. "Well, I guess that's the end of our little talk," he said, and left the cottage, slamming the back door closed.

Dinner was awkward for David, but Laura, traitor that she was, took to Kathleen instantly. She practically threw herself at her. "Come down to the water," she begged, wrapping her hand in Kathleen's and dragging her out the door, Lin in tow. "I want to show you my frog."

"Kathleen seems okay," said Bill.

"Based on what?" David replied sarcastically.

He was determined not to like his father's girlfriend, so he ignored her, although ignoring Kathleen wasn't the easiest thing in the world. She told funny stories, she laughed a lot, and even though she couldn't cook, she chopped vegetables, set the table and created the sort of comfortable atmosphere that David secretly longed for.

"Can I watch you take off your makeup?" Laura asked at bedtime. "My mum doesn't wear makeup, but I'm going to when I grow up."

"Better yet," replied Kathleen, "why don't I give you and Lin a beauty make-over in the morning? I've got everything we'll need: mascara, eye shadow, lipstick, foundation, perfume. I even have mud masks!"

"Yay!" the girls screamed.

"What kind of a person wears makeup at a cottage?" David muttered to Bill.

Dad's eyebrows creased together. "David," he warned.

"Come on, Bill. Let's go play blackjack on the top bunk. Night, everyone." He and Bill had everything they needed in his room: books, a CD player, cards, games and piles of comics.

◗

That night, Kathleen slept in the guest room, so David had one less reason to hate her. It took him a long time to manage to tell Bill about the abrupt change in their summer plans. Just before they fell asleep, he kicked the bottom of Bill's mattress.

"Hey. Quit it." Bill tossed a comic onto the lower bunk.

"We're not hanging around this summer," David said into the darkness.

"Who's we? Quit kicking my bed."

"Laura and me. We're going out west … to some island, to stay with my aunt."

"I didn't know you had an aunt. How long are you going for?"

"I don't know," David lied. "Maybe July, maybe the whole summer. If we like it, we'll stay. If we don't, we'll come home."

Bill rolled over onto his stomach and yawned. "When did you decide to do this?"

David knew Bill must be hurt. "We've been talking about it for a while, but Dad said not to say anything until it was a sure thing. He said it was definite just before dinner."

Bill tossed restlessly above David. "I thought we had plans." He spoke in a quiet monotone.

"Yeah, I know, but sometimes plans have to change."

Plans. David closed his eyes. Who cared about his plans? He rolled over and tried to empty his mind, but all he could think about was what a mess his life was, and there was nothing he could do about it. He'd always wanted to go to the West Coast, but he'd never wanted to be sent away. No matter how he looked at it, this was exactly what was happening to him.

For the rest of the weekend, David avoided contact with both his father and Kathleen, and spent his time out in the canoe with Bill. True to his nature, Bill had not held a grudge about David going away. Although there was no longer any point in discussing the summer ahead, they both kept forgetting. Their conversations were often halted midway by such innocent words as, "Next week we'll …" or "Why don't we put a motor on the canoe?" or "We should build a fort at the base of the cliffs …"

By noon Sunday, David had had enough. He ached to go home, even though it meant saying goodbye to his cottage, the place he loved most in the world.

Chapter Three

THEY'D arrived at their father's apartment in the late afternoon, after dropping Lin and Bill off at their homes. David stood at the window of the room he shared with Laura. Below him, the leafy canopy of the old chestnut tree swayed in the breeze. He longed to be outside, instead of stuck inside the cramped two-bedroom high-rise.

Behind him, Laura busily arranged his sleeping bag on the floor, "Because," she'd explained the first time they'd stayed over, "I'm the youngest and I should get the bed."

Already, she'd reclined her doll, Susie, gracefully on the pillow, her plastic legs wrapped in a worn fuzzy baby blanket that had covered two generations of their family and looked like it.

"Just keep that doll away from me," David said irritably.

The apartment was small enough for David to know exactly what his father was doing at any given time. Right now, for example, he was in the tiny kitchen whistling "Baby Beluga" (as if they were two-year-olds) and cooking spaghetti. David thought his father's tuneless rendition of the popular children's song was a flimsy cover for a guy who must feel like he's walking through a minefield without a metal detector.

"I wish he would shut up with that song. This whole thing is just a joke," David complained.

"I think this is fun, like camping or going to a hotel. You're just in a bad mood 'cause Kathleen likes me better than she does you. That's because I'm nice to her," Laura added.

"Yeah, and you don't have any idea of what's going on here. What do you think is going to happen this summer with Mum and Dad living apart, Kathleen on the scene, and us out of the way on some island off the West Coast? Did you ever stop to think of that? Huh?" David turned away from Laura, fighting back tears.

"You're mean." Laura faced him, her tightly clenched fists hidden by the ridiculous frill on the pink tutu she'd changed into.

David studied his sister's face warily. Her expression reminded him of the canaries he'd once read about. They accompanied coal miners deep into the earth as an early warning sign of danger. A dead canary meant a shortage of oxygen in the mine — time to get out. Laura's trembling lower lip was David's alarm — trouble lay ahead unless he did something fast. A temper tantrum in this little place would be awful; besides, if all of this was hard for him, it must be equally hard for Laura.

"Come on kids, dinner," their father called from the tiny kitchenette.

Laura stood rooted to the ground, her lip warming up to a full quiver. Outside, a chipmunk scurried up the tree trunk, his cheeks fat with nuts.

"I guess I was being mean," David conceded. "What do you say I tell you a story when we're in bed?" He forced a smile, and it didn't feel so bad.

Chameleon-like, Laura lit up immediately. Her lower lip retracted and her hands clapped. Mission accomplished.

"Daddy! David's going to tell me ghost stories tonight. He promised!"

She peeled into the living room. David followed slowly, catching a whiff of garlic and tomatoes. He was hungry — lunch seemed a long time ago.

"David, can I interest you in a piece of your dad's world-famous, too-good-to-be-true garlic toast?"

Their father was a large man. He stood by the table, a cookie tray in hand, loaded down with perfectly browned chunks of French bread. He wore a tattered apron. David squinted at the words scrawled across the front: "OLD EST OOK," he read aloud.

His dad straightened up and the wrinkles in the apron disappeared. "WORLD'S BEST COOK," he corrected, smiling. "Kathleen gave it to me."

It was a lie, like everything else. Their father had never cooked a single meal in all the years he'd lived at home. If he was the world's best at anything, it was not apparent to David. Still, the garlic toast smelled great.

"Sure," David said. "I'll have two pieces, for now."

The OLD EST OOK grinned.

"I want a piece of too-good-to-be-true garlic toast," Laura enthused, plonking down onto her chair.

"One piece for the young lady, and one, I assume, for Susie?" Laura grinned and Dad flipped two pieces of warm toast off the tray onto Laura's plate, pirouetted and deposited another two slices before David.

"I hope," he said, "you are both really hungry because I made a mountain of spaghetti."

"A mountain of spaghetti," Laura laughed, "would fill the whole room!"

"A mountain of spaghetti," Dad answered, "would fill the whole apartment."

David rolled his eyes. Another stupid old game. Why had he ever thought it so hilarious?

"You're silly, Daddy," said Laura.

Their playful banter floated around David, who maintained a calculated silence. Why was it so much easier for his dad to be happy here, away from home?

David was hungry and the spaghetti *was* good, but he ate little, tasting betrayal with every swallow. Always in the back of his mind was his mother, at home, curled on her bed, staring up at her cracked ceiling, her eyes red and swollen. What made her so sad all the time?

"Is Rose staying with your mother tonight, too?" asked his dad, as if reading David's thoughts.

"She usually stays until after dinner on Sundays," replied David shortly.

Halfway through dinner the phone rang. David leapt up from his chair. It might be Mum. "Hello." He grabbed the receiver before the end of the first ring. Silence.

"*Hello*?" he repeated.

"Hello, David. It's Kathleen. Is your father there, please?" Her voice was warm maple syrup — all thick and drippy.

"He's in the middle of dinner. Why don't you call back later, or in the morning?" *Or never.*

Kathleen sighed. "I only need to talk to him for a minute. Please go and get him, David." David smiled at the irritation that had crept into her voice.

"Daaad!" he yelled into the receiver. "Someone for you. I tried to tell her you were busy eating, but she won't listen."

His father appeared beside him. "You don't have to shout like that." He didn't pick up the phone, just fixed his dark eyes on David, who stared back with hostility, until finally, his father looked away. "Go and finish your dinner," he ordered.

"Hello? Oh, hi, Kathleen. Hold on for a minute will you?" He covered the mouthpiece and turned to his son. "If you can't answer the phone politely, leave it alone. I'll take it in my room."

David swallowed quickly and shrugged indifferently, although the anger in his dad's voice strung like a slap in the face. "Whatever, Dad."

"We can talk about this later if you like," said his father, more kindly.

David smiled. A thin, icy smile. No way. David had no intention of making it that easy for him.

"No, we don't need to talk about it," he said. "I just thought it might be Mum calling. She needs us. But you know that."

His father's shoulders dropped and a look of pain flitted across his features. "Hang up the phone for me when I've picked it up in my room," he said, and disappeared down the short hallway. The bedroom door clicked softly shut.

David pressed the phone to his ear. "Hello, Kath," his father said. "Did you get home safely?"

"Mmm," replied Kathleen. "David's still giving you a hard time, I see."

"He'll come around."

"I hope so, John. Right now he's acting like a ... Did he hang up?"

David scooted over to the table, and shovelled a second helping of spaghetti onto his plate just as his father appeared around the corner. Glancing at the receiver lying off the hook, he said, "You forgot to hang up the phone."

"Oops. Sorry, Dad. This spaghetti is almost as good as Mum's."

◖

David considered his spider. He thought that when he got home, he might place a few wood bugs in front of her hole in case she was hungry. Or maybe not. Spoiling her was unwise; she mustn't forget how to hunt on her own. She must not depend on him solely for her food supply; rather, she should think of him as a sort of spider ice-cream man, who dropped by unexpectedly with a plump wood bug or a fat housefly to complement her diet.

"Bloody traffic! We haven't moved half a block in ten minutes." His father's mood had not improved after last night's phone call from Syrup Voice, a.k.a. Kathleen.

They'd been crawling up Yonge Street for half an hour, victims of the closing of the Bay Bloor Extension. Road repairs were a sure sign of the beginning of summer in Toronto.

As usual, David found himself stuck in the back seat. Laura's endless whining had won her front seat action. Well, he preferred it this way. Better that than sitting up front and pretending everything was okay between him and his father.

Fifteen minutes later, their small black car pulled into the driveway. David peered up at their house. It looked vacant, deserted. Sections of the unread *Saturday Star* lay scattered about the porch and front yard. Why hadn't someone cancelled the weekend paper? No one read it anymore.

"I'll just pop in for a moment," said their father, climbing out of the car.

"Yay! Daddy's coming in," Laura squealed. David said nothing, hiding his relief behind an indifferent shrug.

"Don't forget your stuff, Laura." David had become an expert at keeping track of their weekend bags. "And make sure you don't leave Susie in the car." Once, in the beginning, she'd forgotten Susie, and David had wasted his whole morning reassuring his sister that the stupid doll would be safe without her until after school.

Their father lifted the old gate and pushed it open — its hinges long rusted and broken. He cursed. "Everything's falling apart around here. Hurry up. I'll give you five minutes to grab your stuff. I'll drop you off at school on my way to work."

In the wild garden, last week's laundry hung limply in the dead air — the white sheets streaked with dirt. David stooped and picked up a stone from the driveway. It was not perfectly round or flat. He curled his fist until its sharp edges bit into his skin. He hurled it at the sheets, grinning with satisfaction when it hit its target. "Mum forgot to take the laundry in again," he observed.

Laura moved in closer to her brother until her small body pressed against him. He reached for her hand. Their father sighed and walked determinedly down the path. He held his key out in front of him like a shield. David and Laura followed, dragging their feet over the loose bricks.

On the second tread, David paused, looking for his wolf spider, but she wasn't visible. It didn't matter. He had nothing to give her.

The back door was unlocked. A heavy silence greeted them. "Hit the lights, David," his father commanded as if a mere hundred watts could make a difference to the bleak atmosphere.

"We're home, Elizabeth!" he called into the emptiness.

There was no response.

"She can't hear you. Her door is always shut. We have to go up." David attacked the stairs two at a time, noisily, so she would not be surprised.

"Mum, it's us," he announced loudly. *She's not here,* his instinct cried out. He pushed the thought away and opened the bedroom door. The room was, as he'd known it would be, perfectly empty.

The bed had been made, each corner tucked in neatly, the pillows fluffed, the cover smooth and straight. It looked as if it belonged in the display window of a linen store. It looked like it belonged anywhere but in their house. The very thought of his mother making her bed, or any bed for that matter, would be funny if it weren't so ludicrous.

He stepped back over the threshold and pulled the door gently shut behind him. Downstairs he could now hear the low murmur of voices — adult voices — the hushed and flat tones they use when something is really serious. There was another sound too: Laura sniffling. He moved to the top of the stairs and listened to their words.

"I tried to call you, John, but I couldn't reach you." David recognized the voice of his mother's best friend.

"It's okay, Rosa. I'm so glad you were here for her."

"I didn't know what else to do. She refused to eat all weekend and she couldn't stop crying. It was as if her whole world came crashing down around of her. I called her doctor last night and he said I should take her to the hospital."

"You did the right thing." David's father sounded defeated.

"The right thing — whatever that is. I just wish I knew how to help her."

"You and everyone else. You did the best you could. Thank you for staying and waiting for us."

"It's the least I can do. I guess it's back to the experts now."

"Yes," his father agreed. "Somehow all of this will work out. It has to, for the kids. Maybe she'll get the help she needs now."

David sank to the floor, holding onto the hope in the words, but he knew there was no Santa, no Tooth Fairy, and help was way too late for his family.

After Rosa had left, after their father had returned from fetching his clothes, after he had spent what seemed like hours on the phone, after they had eaten a nearly silent dinner, after Laura had been tucked in and the house regained its dreary silence, only then did David allow himself to cry. News of their mother was sparse but reassuring. She'd be okay. She'd stay in the hospital for the next little while. She'd be okay, the doctors promised. Dad would stay in the house until they left for the West Coast. Everything would be fine.

Why, then, did David feel so afraid? Adrift, without a map or a compass in a strange, unnavigable land.

Chapter Four

THE "Fasten Seat Belts" sign blinked on as Laura climbed across her brother, and resettled herself into her seat. "I don't know why you wanted the window seat," grumbled David. "You've hardly sat down for the whole flight."

"What are you? The seat cop?" his sister snapped back at him. "You get the window seat on the way home and you can do what you like with it, so leave me alone."

Before David could retort, the PA crackled to life. "We are about to begin our final approach into Vancouver International Airport. Please ensure your seat belts are fastened securely and your seat backs are in the upright position. The temperature on the ground is seventeen degrees Celsius and local time is eleven in the morning, Pacific time. Thank you for flying with us and enjoy your stay in Vancouver."

Still set on Toronto time, David's watch read two in the afternoon. The watch his dad had given him for his fourteenth birthday. He closed his eyes and an image of his mother appeared unbidden — his mother in her room, curled up on her bed in the semi-darkness, her eyes wide open, staring at the web of cracks fanning across the ceiling. There had been a time when David had wanted to know what shapes she saw in the old plaster, but that, along with hoping for dinner, trying to make his mother smile, and wondering why she was always so sad, had been replaced by hopelessness and uncertainty.

Beneath his feet, the plane shuddered, and Laura jumped. "It's only the captain lowering the gear to get ready for landing," David explained, jarred back to the present by the noisy vibration.

"I know," Laura claimed, looking decidedly relieved.

"Move back, Laura, so I can see, too," David said, craning his neck toward the ridge of mountains that rose out of the coastal city. It was July, but the peaks were still dusted in snow. Shimmering white sails, tugboats and log booms flecked the huge body of water that nudged up against the airport. He was torn between surveying the high country and the low.

The plane touched the runway lightly and taxied toward the ramp. David experienced a mixture of excitement and sadness. The resentment he felt toward his dad for sending them away hadn't lessened, but he felt a strong sense of relief at the same time.

"Do you think Aunt Jennifer will recognize us?" Laura interrupted, unlatching her seat belt and standing up the moment the plane stopped.

"Of course she will. Mum sends her pictures every Christmas and birthday. Have you put your watch on Vancouver time yet? It's three hours behind."

Laura sat back down. "I'm keeping my watch on Toronto time."

"That's …" Stupid, he was about to say, but the look on her face silenced him. "Are you okay, Laura?" he asked instead.

"I'm fine," she replied. "I just want to keep track of what Mum is doing."

David closed his eyes. All around him passengers prepared to deplane. He just wanted to block out the chaos. In Toronto, it was after lunchtime, but Toronto did not exist for him anymore. He reset his watch to 11:12 a.m. Pacific time.

Aunt Jennifer was waiting for them at Arrivals, firmly planted beside the luggage carousel. She greeted them with an enormous grin that reached all the way up to her large green eyes, the same expressive eyes that she shared with their mother. There, however, the resemblance ended. Aunt Jennifer's hair was cropped boyishly short and she wore faded jeans and a T-shirt boasting that "Wild Salmon Don't Do Drugs." *She dresses like a kid*, thought David. *A big kid.* She was at least three sizes larger than their slight mother, but not overweight. She looked like someone who writes cookbooks should look. Her healthy bronze face was devoid of makeup.

"Welcome to Vancouver, David, Laura," she said. "Any of these bags belong to you two?" The three of them waited in silence, watching the luggage descend the conveyer belt, until their own backpacks tumbled into sight. Aunt Jennifer didn't cluck, didn't make small talk, just stood quietly beside them.

"I think she might be all right," David whispered to Laura, partly to convince himself and partly to make Laura feel better.

"She's different from Mum," said Laura. "Did you notice how she dresses?"

"Dad said Aunt Jennifer is a real character," replied David. "I think that might be a good thing."

They exited the busy terminal, but rather than going to the parking lot, their aunt hailed a bright yellow cab.

"South Terminal!" she boomed at the driver.

Laura giggled. "She's so loud!" she whispered.

"I know what you mean," David agreed, "compared to Mum." In a flash he was back in Toronto. Evening time outside, the sun had set and the grey night slid in through the windows, filling the old house with shadows. He and Laura sat motionless in front of the TV, their faces pale in the flickering light. They waited in mutual understanding for the soft tread of their mother's footsteps on the stairs. Still, they didn't hear her when she arrived.

"I'm sorry," she breathed in the faraway voice they had become accustomed to. "I must have slept."

She smiled wanly and David willed himself to smile back. He pretended not to notice her red-rimmed eyes — eyes always on the brink of tears.

"David!" Laura elbowed him hard in the ribs. "David is always somewhere else," she explained to Aunt Jennifer.

"Good for you," Aunt Jennifer winked. She opened the cab door. "Hop in," she said.

They complied and the taxi rolled away from the curb. Aunt Jennifer chatted to the driver, while David and Laura sat in expectant silence. In their experience, adults preferred quiet kids.

"Where are we going?" Laura finally blurted out, curiosity triumphing over politeness.

"I thought you'd never ask. The float-plane dock," Aunt Jennifer replied. "It takes seven hours, two ferries and a speedboat to drive to Bliss Landing. We'll be there in less than an hour in a float plane."

"Muskoka, where we go in the summer, is only two hours out of Toronto," Laura said.

"*Used* to go," David mumbled. He stared out the car window at the feathery clouds that hovered over the peaks of the mountain range to the north. To the south, the mighty Fraser River snaked along beside them, stained a muddy brown by tons of silt. Fishing boats pushed upstream against the strong current.

They drove beside the river until they reached a wooden building perched on stilts, leaning out over the fast-moving water. Beside the building, a small float plane bobbed up and down in the gentle waves. The cab lurched into the gravel parking lot and skidded to a stop under a rustic sign, "The Flying Beaver."

"I get it. Beaver as in plane, not animal," David said.

"Exactly!" bellowed Aunt Jennifer. "Everyone out." She threw open the cab door. "I hope neither of you kids gets motion sickness. Let's go! We have a plane to catch."

David hoisted his backpack onto his shoulders. Laura leapt out of the car. "Get mine, too," she called to David, her eyes already on the dock.

"Oh, brother," he complained, reaching to retrieve the pink and blue pack.

They were going on a float plane! He'd seen float planes land on the lake at Muskoka, but he'd never been on one. It was the coolest thing in the world!

"You go ahead, David, and leave Laura's bag. She can get it herself. Go on down to the wharf and let Paul know we're here. Paul is the pilot — he's expecting us. Laura and I will be down in a jiffy." Aunt Jennifer smiled, her eyes on Laura, her voice firm.

"Sure." David grinned. He stuck out his tongue at his sister and hurried down the boardwalk, propelled by his own heavy backpack. Suddenly David skidded on the wet ramp, losing his footing on the slimy, green-speckled wood. In a flash, his sneaker slid out from under him and he lost his balance, careening backward, his arms flailing helplessly over his head. He landed on his back on the floating dock with a thud.

"Ouch!" he exclaimed. "Right on my tailbone!"

"What do we have here? Looks to me like a big sea turtle caught the wrong way up." A large strong hand accompanied the deep voice. "Are you in a hurry to get somewhere, young man? One, two, three and up."

David took the outstretched hand and quickly found himself planted solidly on his feet again. He looked into the eyes of a tall, dark-haired grinning man. He wore a crisp white shirt, decorated by four yellow bars. The pilot.

"Thanks," David said.

"You're David, right? I'm Paul Jansen. I've been expecting you. Jenn's nephew from the other side of the Rocks."

"Rocks?" David asked, rubbing his throbbing elbow.

"You know. The Rocky Mountains. You're from Toronto. Back East. The Heartland. Central Canada." Paul's eyes danced over David, filled with mischievous humour.

"Yeah, uh, I guess, the Rocks, that's me. Aunt Jennifer said to tell you she'll be here in a minute. With my sister," David added.

"Don't want to forget her. Or do we?" Paul joked. "You ever been on a seaplane before? No. It will be the best thing you ever did. This one is a Beaver — seats six plus the pilot. Hey, how'd you like to sit up front with me? You can be my co-pilot. How's your eyesight?"

Paul did not wait for answers and his enthusiasm was contagious.

"No. No. Yes. Good." David laughed, following Paul over to where the plane was secured to the wharf by a thick yellow rope.

"If you've got your sea legs back, hop onto the float and up into the front seat. I'll stow your bag in the float."

"Really," David said. "I can go in?"

"It's not safe to fly sitting on the wing," Paul joked, as he stowed David's bag securely into the float plane's pontoon.

David climbed up the steep steps into the plane. It was an older airplane, not streamlined and sleek like the big jet they had flown in from Toronto. He was careful to climb into his seat without bumping the controls in the middle. David peered out the small window. Docked, the nose of the Beaver pointed up, making it difficult to see much except the scattered white clouds dotting the overcast sky.

Wait till he told Bill about this! He finished the adjustments to his seat belt and figured out the shoulder harness seconds before Aunt Jennifer and Laura climbed into the back of the plane. Laura's dark frown reflected her displeasure at having to carry her own backpack. Her protruding lip brought a fleeting grin to David's face.

"No fair," she whined. "How come David gets the front seat? I always get the front seat."

"Not today." Paul eased his bulky body in beside David, patting Aunt Jennifer's leg affectionately as he squeezed by her.

"Oh, Paul," she flushed, but David saw her pleased smile. "Put these on, kid." Paul tossed David a headset. "Way to go — you even knew to get into the right seat. If everyone is buckled in, we're outta here like a homesick angel!"

"Off we go!" shouted Aunt Jennifer. "Home to Desolation Sound."

The engine droned to life and the small plane bumped off downriver until it gathered enough speed to lift off the Fraser and climb into the sky.

At 1000 metres, the Beaver shot through the scattered cloud into radiant sunshine. David closed his eyes and let the solar warmth wash over him. This was flying! The small plane vibrated gently as it hummed across the blue sky, still climbing.

At 1600 metres, the Beaver levelled off. David opened his eyes and glanced over at the pilot. "I …" he stuttered. "This is …"

Paul's weathered face crinkled. "Awesome, isn't it? As soon as I've finished my after-takeoff check, we can sit back and enjoy the ride."

David thought fleetingly about the other place — the world below this world — where parents fought and people cried. He thought about unnaturally quiet houses, cramped apartments and lugging his backpack from one end of Toronto to the other. He thought about it in a big watered-down version, the images diluted, and he felt nothing beyond a reassurance that none of it could touch him up here between heaven and earth.

"I could stay here forever," he said.

"Not in this plane. Three hours max. Besides, no bathrooms." Paul winked and lowered his voice, even though the others couldn't hear him without headsets. "But I know what you mean, kid."

David knew instinctively that Paul told the truth. He could see that Paul and Aunt Jennifer were not the kind of adults who said things they didn't mean.

Laura reached over the back of David's seat and tapped him impatiently on his shoulder. He knew that to ignore her would be useless. Exasperated, he pulled off his earphones. "What?" He had to yell to make himself heard.

"I have to go to the bathroom!" said Laura.

"You'll have to hold it for a little longer," Aunt Jennifer replied, before David could snap back at his sister. Gently but firmly, she pulled Laura back into her seat. "Put your headset back on, David. Laura, if you have a problem, you're allowed to talk to me. In fact, I'd prefer if you did."

David let out the breath he hadn't been aware he'd been holding.

Paul checked his watch. "About twenty minutes longer, to be exact," he said. "I'm going to begin my descent."

"Back into the clouds," David remarked.

"It's usually pretty clear over the Sound," Paul said, flicking gauges as they approached their destination. David appreciated that Paul didn't ask him to be quiet while he checked his charts and instruments. Finally, somebody gave him some credit for brains.

For David, the flight represented the quickest forty-five minutes he'd ever known. As they neared Desolation Sound, the clouds thinned, just as Paul had predicted they would.

"There's a halo of light over the whole area," he told David. "It can be low overcast everywhere else on the coast, and clear as a jellyfish in moonlight over the Sound."

David had never seen a jellyfish at all, and especially not in moonlight, but he knew exactly what the pilot meant.

"David! I *really* have to go to the bathroom." Laura planted her foot firmly on the back of David's seat and pushed as hard as she could.

Impatiently, David lifted the headset off one ear and turned to his sister, but Aunt Jennifer met his eyes: *I'll take care of it.*

"You only have two options here, Laura — go or wait — but please take your foot off your brother's seat."

David sighed and turned back in his seat. If Laura was acting like a spoiled brat, it was as much his fault as hers. He babied her — better that than fight with her. He'd done his best, but he was tired of her and her stupid doll, and all her demands.

Out the window, the gap between the Beaver and the ocean had narrowed. They were only about a hundred metres off the water. Paul pointed to a large island that lay off the right wing, "There's Hernando."

"Orcas at one o'clock!" Aunt Jennifer shouted.

David looked at Paul, puzzled. Aunt Jennifer spoke her own language.

Paul laughed. "Just out your front window and to the right there's a pod of killer whales. See them? Hold on."

He banked the plane sharply right. "We don't want to get too close. Three hundred metres is the limit, and I don't even like to do that." Laura squealed, her discomfort forgotten. Directly below them, four huge black and white whales sliced in and out of the grey-green water. The sun glinted off their magnificent bodies.

"Look, David! Beluga whales!" Laura shrieked.

"No belugas on this coast, except at the aquarium. Those are killer whales, travelling north for the summer," Paul explained.

He gave David the thumbs-up sign. "Seeing a killer whale is good luck." He paused before adding, "Unless you happen to be a salmon!"

The whales were gone as quickly as they had appeared. "They can stay underwater for about twenty minutes," Paul explained, "and in that time, they can sure travel a good distance." Only a few boats were visible near where the whales had been, bobbing in the flat water.

"Whale watchers at twelve o'clock!" Aunt Jennifer thumped Paul on the shoulders. He took off his headset, and David did the same, curious to hear their conversation. "Buzz them, that should scare them off."

"Relax, Jenn, I'm not buzzing anyone. I plan to keep my job for a while, and I'd do as much harm to the whales as I'd do to any humans. Anyway, that's Johnny Taylor's outfit. He's a decent guy and he runs a good operation. He'd sooner hurt himself than endanger a whale."

"Why do you want to scare them off, Aunt Jennifer?" asked Laura.

"They're harassing the pod. They never leave them alone, constantly chasing them so they can get a photo for their landlubber clients."

"Leave it for now, Jenn," said Paul calmly. "The kids haven't even arrived on the island. No politics." To David, he added, "Your aunt thinks all whale-watching operations are bad news, but it just isn't true. Problem is that one bad apple spoils the barrel."

"Bliss Cove ahead!" Aunt Jenn hollered, demurring to Paul. She pointed to a small island in the middle of the narrow strait.

Paul banked right and circled the Beaver over the land mass. Fern Island was shaped like a jagged half moon and was about five kilometres long, smaller than most of the surrounding islands. Trees taller and greener than David had ever imagined smothered its surface, but it was the beaches that hooked him.

"It looks like Hawaii!" he exclaimed.

"Better than Hawaii," Aunt Jennifer protested. "No crowds. The beach belongs to us."

Wide sandy beaches bordered the entire island, the colour of unbleached flour. From the air, the water surrounding Fern appeared sapphire blue and crystal clear. A few cabins were visible, peeking out of the trees. Pleasure boats rocked gently offshore.

Paul eased the plane down expertly until its pontoons kissed the water with a slight bump. They skidded across the surface, losing speed, and came to a stop centimetres from the wharf.

"Perfect, as always," Aunt Jennifer said, undoing her seat belt.

"Please remain in your seats with your seat belts buckled until the plane comes to a full stop," Laura intoned. They all laughed, even David.

"That's odd, there's no one out to greet us," said Paul, surveying the empty beach.

"It's the beginning of the season," said Aunt Jennifer.

While David held onto the mooring rope and Paul unloaded their bags and some plastic boxes, Aunt Jennifer grabbed Laura's hand. She brushed her lips over Paul's cheek lightly before she made a beeline for the woods.

"Got to get to the bathroom," she called over her shoulder.

"Thanks for the ride, Paul. See you next week, if not sooner."

"Aunt Jennifer," David said, "moves incredibly fast for a grown-up."

Paul laughed. "That's for sure," he agreed. "Greased lightning."

"Are you leaving?" David didn't try to hide the disappointment he felt.

"Yes. I have to pick up some passengers on Savary and head back to Vancouver. I come back here every Friday, unless I get a charter trip. They call me the Daddy plane because I drop off the dads on Friday and take them back to Vancouver to work on Monday." He reached out and grasped David's hand. "You're a good kid. I guess I'll be seeing lots of you this summer."

Feeling awkward, David looked away toward the forest. At home, in Toronto, adults were different. Dad said you shouldn't get too friendly with people you hardly knew. Would that include this pilot? No. He wasn't just any old pilot — he was Paul, who knew all about whales and treating kids right.

David looked into Paul's kind brown eyes. "Thanks for the ride," he said. "I guess I'll see you around … I mean I hope so."

Paul climbed back into the Beaver, pulled the door shut and poked his head out the cockpit window. "Push me off, kid, when I give you the sign. And David, try to make yourself visible when I fly in next time. Maybe I can take you for a ride."

The cockpit window slid shut and the propeller whirred to life. Paul turned and gave David the thumbs-up. David put all his might into pushing the small plane toward the open ocean, then he stood and watched it climb high into the sky.

"Bye, Paul," he whispered, long after the Beaver had been swallowed by the clouds.

Chapter Five

DAVID plonked himself down on his backpack, surrounded by seven large plastic containers. *Jenn M* was scrawled on each one in thick black marker.

"Don't want to mix them up with other people's," Aunt Jennifer had explained. "Most of us islanders shop in Vancouver. It's a lot cheaper than Lund, the little village across the water, although you won't find better cinnamon buns or pies anywhere else on the West Coast."

David felt he could easily eat ten cinnamon buns right now. Paul had dropped them off on a large wooden wharf that floated, at low tide, three metres below the pier leading to the beach. The ramp connecting the two climbed at a sharp angle, and David contemplated dragging all their supplies to the top. Beneath his feet, the water rose and fell rhythmically. His heavy cargo pants, the ones his dad had insisted he wear on the flight out, were hot and itchy. He wanted to take them off. The sea looked inviting and he knelt down, dipping his hand into the salty water. It was cool, much cooler than lake water, and prickled his skin.

A metre in front of him, a head popped out of the water. "Yikes!" David jerked his hand away, shocked to find himself staring into the bulging, silvery eyes of a sleek grey seal. The seal eyed him back curiously. David laughed. "Hi, there," he said. The seal dove out of sight.

"Who are you talking to?" Laura called from the top of the ramp.

"There's a seal out there," David replied, "close enough to touch. At least, I think it's a seal."

"Where?" Laura dropped the battered old wheelbarrow she'd brought back with her and rushed down the ramp to see for herself.

"He dove under. You probably scared him."

"I did not," Laura protested. "Anyway, Aunt Jennifer says we have to fill the wheelbarrow with our stuff and take it up to the cabin. It's just above the beach in the woods."

They were only able to fit two plastic containers into the wheelbarrow at a time, so it took David and Laura four trips to move everything up the ramp.

The path, more of a deer track really, rose steeply from the shoreline, where it disappeared into the huge old cedars before winding around a craggy boulder and stopping abruptly at the wide porch. In the end, the kids found it easier to unload the heavy bins from the wheelbarrow at the foot of the path and carry them the rest of the way to the cabin, rather than try to balance them in the wheelbarrow over the uneven terrain.

The cabin stood in a small clearing surrounded by ferns; their feathery tips equalled David in height. "Hence the name, Fern Island," explained Aunt Jennifer, standing in the doorway.

The Pacific was clearly visible from the cabin's ample windows. A gnarly red-brown tree grew up through a hole cut in the middle of the cabin's sunwashed deck. The tree's bark was smooth and soft. "It's called an arbutus tree," Aunt Jennifer said. "They only grow on the West Coast."

"Just put the containers right here," Aunt Jennifer directed, pointing to the top of the stairs, "and as soon as you're finished, we'll eat."

"David usually cooks," said Laura, "but he only ever gives me peanut butter sandwiches for lunch. I'm sick of them."

"That's not true. Besides, why don't you make your own lunch once in a while?" said David. "You're eleven, not six."

"Didn't your mum cook sometimes?" asked Aunt Jennifer, pulling a bag of apples out of one container. "If my memory serves me right, she's a wonderful cook."

"Come on, Laura, one more trip and we're finished." David took Laura by the arm and directed her down the path. "You better not say anything bad about Mum," he warned her.

Laura glared at him and ran ahead. David walked slowly down to the wharf to where his sister lay on her stomach, dangling both arms into the water.

"I can see you're going to be a big help," he said. "Why don't you go back to the cabin? I'll bring up the last one."

Once alone, he sat down on a blue plastic container. In the distance, across the water, and nestled into a protected cove, was the small village of Lund, but in his imagination he saw their silent, empty kitchen in Toronto. David blinked rapidly, afraid if he started to cry, he might not stop. There were so many contradictions. His mother *had been* a good, no, a great cook. She'd been fun, too. Was it somehow his fault that she'd changed so much? Did she miss him as much as he missed her? Did she even notice he was gone? And if she did, did it bother her? Once he would have been sure of the answer to that question. Now he wasn't.

He sat for a while, lost in his thoughts, hoping in vain for the seal to reappear. When it didn't, David picked up the last container, shoved it into the wheelbarrow and headed for the cabin.

Beneath his feet, the spongy path yielded to his weight; it was like walking on extra firm jelly. The trees crowded up against it, blocking out the light. It was all so different from the cottage in Muskoka: beautiful, but not the same. David fought back a wave of homesickness.

Aunt Jennifer waited for him at the top of the path. She thrust a can of ice-cold Coke into his hands. "It is a bit overwhelming at first," she said. "Take a break and have a look around. I'll call you when lunch is ready."

"No fair. I'm thirsty. I helped, too," Laura whined. She reached for David's Coke.

David groaned. "Shut up, Laura. Here." He handed her his drink. She stuck her tongue out at him, plonked herself down into the nearest chair, tilted her head back and proceeded to enjoy his pop.

"A thank-you might be nice," David demanded.

"Thank you," said Laura, in her sweetest voice.

Aunt Jennifer frowned at Laura and dug into her deep pocket. "There is plenty more where that came from. From now on, Laura, if you want a drink, you can ask me or help yourself out of the fridge. There's a recycling bin for cans just outside the back door."

Laura nodded. At least she had the good grace to blush. David smiled tentatively at his aunt. "Lucky for you, I have a fridge in my pocket." She held out another can of pop to him.

"Thanks," David said grinning. "Cool pockets."

Her face crinkled into a wide smile. "Follow me. I'll show you where your rooms are," she said kindly.

She skipped across the porch. "Come on." She slid open the sliding glass doors to the main house. "Close the screen door, we don't want bugs in here," she called over her shoulder.

"David will," said Laura.

David ignored his sister. "You don't know what bugs are until you spend time in Muskoka."

"You a bug person, David? There's a big old spider that lives under the woodpile. I'll have to introduce you."

"I hate spiders. David has one at home. He feeds it. It's disgusting."

"Be quiet, Laura," muttered David under his breath, and for once, Laura was.

The cabin seemed bigger inside, its massive log walls sunset-coloured. David ran his hand over their hard, cool surface. Books were everywhere. They lined the walls and lay haphazardly in tall stacks beside the chairs and sofas.

"There's a picture of us." Laura ran to the huge stone fireplace in the living room. On top of the gnarled driftwood mantelpiece in a silver frame stood a photo of the Garretts. David looked to be about eight and Laura five. "We look happy," said David. "Even Mum."

"I think she was happy then," Aunt Jennifer said, putting her arm on David's shoulder. He shrugged it off.

"Mum and you don't look at all alike," noted Laura. "Your hair is dark and your eyes are a darker green, almost brown. Mum's blonde, and really thin. She's beautiful."

"Are you going to show us the rest of the house?" interjected David.

"We looked alike when we were younger," Aunt Jennifer joked defensively.

David glared at Laura. "I didn't mean anything by it," said Laura crossly.

Aunt Jennifer smiled. "Of course you didn't. Voilà, the main house." She gestured to a door leading off the living room. "Where I sleep." The small bright bedroom held a large unmade bed by the window, facing east to the water. An old typewriter sat on a battered desk. Above it hung a bulletin board covered in hand-written recipes. "And where I work," added Aunt Jennifer.

"No computer?" said David.

"No computer," confirmed Aunt Jennifer.

"No phone? What if there's an emergency?"

"Not me. The people one bay over have a cell phone."

"Where do we sleep?" asked Laura.

"You two will sleep in the bunkhouse."

The bunkhouse had three bedrooms, each with two bunks. In the middle was an airtight stove and two large overstuffed chairs, the upholstery worn and faded.

"We don't have electricity on the island and all our heat is solar or wood — and then there's the cookstove. You two will be the woodcutters. The woodpile is at the back of the house."

David chose the room facing east, so he could see the sunrise over the water when he woke up.

"I'm sleeping here, too," Laura insisted. "In the top bunk." She unzipped her backpack, pulled out Susie and threw her onto the bed.

"I don't want that stupid doll anywhere near me," David muttered under his breath.

"Laura, we'll put your stuff in the other room," said Aunt Jennifer. "Your mother and I used to share that room in the summers. I think you'll like it." She took Laura by the hand and led her out of the room, winking at David.

He smiled gratefully. Aunt Jennifer was turning out to be an unexpected ally.

"Get changed out of those clothes and come into the main house for lunch," she said. "And no fighting." She launched out of the cabin, pulling the door closed behind her.

"I'm telling. If you call Susie names, I'm telling." Laura called from her bedroom.

"Go ahead!" David shouted back. "I don't think it'll make a huge difference." In truth, he was sick and tired of babysitting Laura. He glanced at his watch. Two o'clock. Even though he'd promised to forget about home, he automatically counted ahead three hours. Five o'clock in Toronto, almost dinnertime, and it wasn't his problem anymore! He smiled.

"What are you laughing at?" Laura appeared in his doorway.

"Nothing."

After a lunch of tuna sandwiches, apples, cookies and fruit tarts all washed down with lemonade, David grabbed his binoculars and tore out of the cabin.

"Back in a while," he called, and disappeared down the path before Laura had a chance to follow him.

He headed down to the pier, his binoculars swinging around his neck, surprised to spot a boy about his own age or maybe a bit younger out on the wharf. David hadn't expected, or even considered, that there might be other kids on Fern Island. The boy's shoeless feet dangled in the water and he balanced a long fishing rod between his bony knees. Beside him sat a pail.

"Hi," David said. "What's in the pail?" He peered in at a collection of submerged shellfish.

The boy reeled in his line and stretched back lazily. He squinted at David upside down and backward. "Mussels," he replied. "What else?"

"What are they for?" David bent down to take a closer look.

"Bait. I shell them first, then I hook them. Hi. I'm Matthew. Who are you?"

"I'm David." David sat down, removed his sandals and stuck

his feet into the water. "I saw a seal right here this morning."

"That was probably Clapper," Matthew said.

"Clapper?"

"Yeah. We call him that because he slaps his flippers on the surface of the water at night, and it sounds like he's clapping."

David nodded. "How do you know it's the same seal?"

Matthew grinned. "I guess we don't." He laughed. "I guess we call them all Clapper. Where are you staying?"

"Up at Jennifer Moffat's place," David replied. "Me and my little sister." He made a face.

The boy lifted his tanned bare feet above his head and pointed his toes at the sky. He pedalled his legs furiously as if he were riding an inverted bicycle.

"Going swimming?" He pedalled in reverse.

David looked at the grey-blue water and thought about Clapper. There were no seals in Muskoka. "Sure," he replied. "In a while."

Matthew pedalled harder. "We're two cabins over. That way." He pointed with his toe. "I have a sister, too. She's nine. I'm escaping her." His legs rotated above him faster. "I knew you were coming today. Jennifer told me and I heard the Daddy plane arrive. Your mum's depressed," he added matter of factly.

"She is not," David snapped. "She's sick, that's all, and it's none of your business." David wanted to kick the boy. He thought about his mum, alone in her room all day and all night. So far away.

"People get sick," he said, taking a deep breath.

"Yup," Matthew agreed. "Hurry up and get your swimsuit. It's hot." He threw a mussel into the water. "And I'm not catching anything. Not even a dog. Fish aren't biting — turning their noses up at my fresh juicy mussels." He plopped a few more over the side. "Do you like fishing?"

"Yeah."

It was not exactly a lie. David knew he would like fishing once he tried it. They'd fished in Pine Lake, or at least thrown their hooks in the water, but the fish were small and there weren't many of them.

Matthew grinned. "Good. A fishing buddy."

"Why would you want to catch a dog?" David asked.

"Not a real dog," laughed Matthew. "A dogfish. They look like little sharks and they eat anything."

David quickly extracted his foot from the water. Whales, seals and now dogfish. What else was in there? "I just have to run up to the cabin and change into my suit. Back in a minute." He took off down the wharf, up the path and skirted around the main house, changing quietly into his swimsuit, on full alert for Laura.

He spotted her in the living room, playing a raucous game of checkers with Aunt Jennifer, and by the sound of her laughter, winning. His aunt saw him as he darted across the porch toward the stairs. Oh, great! David slowed reluctantly. Aunt Jennifer smiled at him. He stared back at her. She winked and waved him on. "Go," she mouthed silently.

"Go?" he mouthed back.

She nodded. He didn't move. "Go on," she mouthed again.

Understanding finally, David scurried behind the arbutus tree and took the stairs in a single bound. Aunt Jennifer was okay. She shouldn't have told Matthew about his mother, but she was still okay.

Matthew lay stretched out in the sun on the wharf. David crept quietly behind him, let out an ear-piercing war cry, and swallowing his fear, cannon-balled into the ocean, soaking his new friend in the process. The chilly water, much colder than he'd expected, sent shock waves through his body. He surfaced and gasped for air.

Matthew stood up and shook himself. "How's the water?"

"It's warm," David lied. "Come on in."

Summertime at last!

The boys spent the rest of the afternoon in and out of the water. David managed to push to the back of his mind his fear of the assortment of creatures who called the sea their home. Matthew turned out to be a real chatterbox. He drew diagrams in the sand to map out the cabins on Fern Island, and stuck a stick in the middle of the ones where kids their age summered. There were only three sticks protruding from the sandy map when he was finished. "Some come on weekends, some for a few weeks, and some like us, for the whole summer," he explained. "How long are you here for?"

David shrugged. "I don't know. Maybe until Labour Day weekend."

"That'd be great!"

By late afternoon when it was time for the boys to return to their cabins, they'd become firm friends, and best of all, David realized, Matthew's little sister was a year younger than Laura. "She's a real pain," said Matthew.

"They'll get along great, then," David replied.

"Why didn't you tell me you were going swimming?" Laura complained at dinner. "I would have gone with you."

"I couldn't find you," David lied. "Besides, I hung out with Matthew."

"More potatoes, David?" Aunt Jennifer dolloped a heap of mashed potatoes onto his plate and added a slab of butter. "Did you meet Matthew Bloom today?"

"Mmm," managed David, his mouth full. He swallowed slowly. "He knew all about us already."

"I told him you and Laura were coming. He was pretty excited. There aren't many kids on Fern."

David put down his fork. He no longer felt like eating. "May I be excused?"

"Of course, David. I'm sure you're both tired. I keep forgetting about the time difference between here and Toronto." Aunt Jennifer smiled at him across the table.

David's mouth suddenly went dry. Unable to make eye contact with his aunt, he stood abruptly. "Are you finished, Laura?" He reached for her plate.

"You can see I'm not. Wait a sec."

David hesitated. He wanted to say something to Aunt Jennifer about privacy. She'd had no right to talk to strangers about his mother, but he couldn't find the words.

"You go ahead, dear," Aunt Jennifer said. "We are *each* quite capable of clearing our own dishes. Feel free to help yourself to a book."

"David hates reading," said Laura. "He never used to, but now he hates everything to do with school."

"Well, if you change your mind, the books are there to read," said his aunt.

"Are you coming, Laura?" David walked toward the sliding door leading to the bunkhouse.

"In a while," she said. She picked up her plate and carried it to the sink.

"Night," said David. "I didn't know you knew how to do dishes!"

"Good night, David," said Aunt Jennifer and she made no attempt to hug him, like so many adults might have.

David lit the coal-oil lamp in his bedroom. A soft yellow glow warmed the room, casting shadows on the thick walls. He wished he'd picked out a book. Laura had been right, he used to love reading and school. His last two report cards were probably both still waiting on the table at home. He hadn't done so well in the last term. One B, four Cs and two C+s. Not that it mattered. No one had read the report anyway.

Cool night air filled the bunkhouse and he snuggled down into his sleeping bag. The last sound David heard before drifting off to sleep was the slap of Clapper's flippers on the still, black water.

◖

He awoke early the next morning to the low throb of outboard motors coming from the direction of the cove. David glanced at his watch. Eight o'clock. Early for him, but in Ontario, he remembered, it was already eleven.

He found Aunt Jennifer in the kitchen, squeezing fresh oranges for breakfast. A kettle simmered on the wood stove.

"Good morning, Aunt Jennifer."

"Bloody tourists!" she snapped, grinding the orange rind. She jerked her head in the general direction of Bliss Cove and the engine sounds.

"What's wrong?" David sat down at the table and rubbed the sleep out of his eyes.

"Nothing," she retorted bleakly, "except for those gawkers out beyond the cove. There's nothing I hate more than waking up to the sound of outboard engines. Grab your binoculars and come out on the porch and I'll show you what they're up to."

There were three boats — an aluminum dinghy, plus two rubber inflatables propelled by large engines and filled to capacity with orange-suited people — men, women and children. Most were armed with either cameras or binoculars.

"What are they doing?" David asked. "What are they wearing?"

"Survival suits," Aunt Jennifer scowled. "They're whale watchers, from the mainland. They come here to take pictures of our resident pod. If you're patient, you'll see them too."

David studied the scene through his glasses. It didn't take long for one, then two, then five huge black and white orcas to appear. They were travelling north toward Johnstone Strait, diving gracefully in and out of the water, their huge bodies startlingly graceful.

Aunt Jennifer sighed. She crossed and recrossed her arms. "Take a good look at them." The 'A' pod, are our resident whales. They won't stick around here too much longer with those idiots harassing them."

David watched the circling boats. He'd like to be out there so close to the huge whales. Only one craft kept its distance, while the other two edged in closer and closer, driving the whales ahead of them. David did not put down his binoculars until the pod and the boats disappeared altogether around the tip of the island. "Whose boat was the old, battered one? The one that hung back?"

"Drifter. Drifter McGee, from Sand Dollar Bay here on Fern. He keeps a close eye on the whale watchers. He doesn't much like people, but he sure loves whales. He used to fish, but not anymore. He turned in his licences."

"I didn't know whale-watching was a bad thing."

"It doesn't have to be and it wasn't always," said Aunt Jennifer, "but now there are too many boats chasing too few whales. The motors are noisy and it stresses the animals. Sometimes I think we're just loving them to death. There are a lot of rules around whale-watching, but not all the operators or private boaters obey them."

"Rules," said David. "Like what?"

"Like don't go any closer to the animals than 100 metres. Like cut your engines because the noise bothers them. Like approach them only from their sides, not their heads or tails. Don't speed across their path or cut them off from the shore, or crowd them into the shore. If they're resting, leave them. Like don't accelerate when you're leaving them until you're 300 metres away." Aunt Jennifer sighed. "Common sense rules, really."

David nodded. He had never thought about it from the whale's point of view before. In fact, after just one day away from everything familiar, he was beginning to think the world was a lot bigger, and a lot more interesting than he'd ever imagined.

Chapter Six

DAVID swung the axe over his head and brought it crashing down on the wedge of fir that balanced precariously on a block of cedar. It ricocheted off the wood and nearly grazed his knee.

"Dead centre," Aunt Jennifer had told him. "Fir is a soft wood, but it's hard to chop. You must hit it exactly in the right place or it won't split."

He swung again. Bull's eye! The log splintered, falling into two perfect pieces at his feet.

"Yes!" Aunt Jennifer bellowed, from where she stood at a safe distance in the clearing.

She stepped forward and offered him a glass of lemonade, which he accepted gratefully. Scattered around him lay a growing pile of cedar, alder and fir.

Nights on Fern Island, even summer nights, were damp and chilly compared to nights in Muskoka. The cold crept beneath your covers and into your dreams, making sleep uncomfortable. Every night, Aunt Jennifer, David or Laura lit the airtight stove so that by bedtime warmth permeated the bunkhouse.

Reluctantly, Laura piled the split wood. "I don't see why I can't chop the wood, too," she complained. "Stacking it is the boring part." She'd interlaced the wood, as Aunt Jennifer had shown her, into three sturdy piles.

"Good work," said Aunt Jennifer. "Stacking is just as important as chopping."

David finished chopping wood and changed into his swimsuit. In the past three weeks, he and Laura had fallen into an easy routine: morning chores included sweeping out their bedrooms, cleaning the woodstove and laying the evening fire. Aunt Jennifer always prepared huge breakfasts of pancakes and bacon, eggs on toast, blueberry muffins or omelettes. Once the dishes were cleared away, washed and dried, David and Laura were free to do as they pleased. It was a lot of work, more than they'd ever had to do before, but neither of them minded — in fact, they enjoyed it.

Two or three mornings a week, after chores, they'd pile into Aunt Jennifer's aluminum boat and motor over to Lund for groceries. That always meant cinnamon buns and hot chocolate. David, under Aunt Jennifer's careful tutelage, soon became a skilled small boat operator. He learned to dock the boat, start and shut down the engine, refuel and secure the boat safely.

"By the end of the summer, you'll be able to go out on your own," Aunt Jennifer promised.

Their father wrote on a regular basis, and they picked up his letters at Aunt Jennifer's post office box. Although Laura usually replied the very afternoon the letters arrived, David had yet to write a word to his father. He'd sent one long letter to Bill, mostly about Clapper and Matthew, and two postcards to his mother, each enthusing about the beauty of Desolation Sound.

"Your mother will be thrilled to get those," Aunt Jennifer said. "Don't forget that as a young girl, this," and Aunt Jennifer spread out her arms, gesturing toward the islands scattered throughout the sound, "this was her playground."

David secretly hoped the pictures on the postcards of breaching whales and crimson sunsets might make his mother better, at least well enough to want to come and spend some time with them on Fern Island.

On the mornings when they didn't boat over to Lund, there was plenty to do on the island. Bliss Cove had been aptly named. At the foot of the path to Aunt Jennifer's cabin, the thick forest opened onto a grassy knoll that fell gently to the long sandy beach. Driftwood in every shape and size provided a continual supply of wonderful beachcombing material. The horseshoe-shaped Bliss Cove faced southeast, and its calm protected waters were ideal for fishing, swimming and wakeboarding.

As small as Aunt Jennifer's boat was, she'd fitted it with the biggest possible motor, and every afternoon, weather permitting, she towed any and all interested kids around the cove on their wakeboards, often handing the job of skipper over to David.

Matthew and David's hope that their sisters would become friends materialized. Laura and Christine were soon inseparable, and for the first time in a long, long time, David didn't feel responsible for Laura's entertainment.

The second day on Fern, Aunt Jennifer had donned her swimsuit and marched Laura and David down to the wharf. The tide rested at its highest point. Despite her size, Aunt Jennifer moved like one of the white-tailed deer that grazed on the knolls and filled the woods. "Follow me," she'd called out. "The only way to get into the ocean is to jump!" She jogged down the pier and leapt into the green water.

David's experience of the day before had made him more wary than usual. He turned to Laura, straightfaced. "After you. It's really warm. Warmer than the lake."

Seconds later, she surfaced, sputtering. "Liar! It's freezing."

"Come on in, David," called Aunt Jennifer. "I need to know how well you can swim before I can comfortably let you loose."

That afternoon, David and Laura's years of swimming lessons paid off. Aunt Jennifer cut through the water with the speed and agility of the seals that occasionally surfaced at a distance. The children followed her, swimming parallel to the beach until their muscles ached and their bodies were numb from the cold sea.

They waded out of the water at the far end of Bliss Cove and lay on the hot white sand. The sun warmed their bodies, and the crystallized salt from the ocean baked onto their skins. "You're both really good swimmers," Aunt Jennifer said approvingly. "You'll be fine in the water, as long as you don't get far from shore and always swim with a buddy. Laura, I think for now you're better off having an adult watch you."

David closed his eyes and let her words float over him. A contented smile played about his lips. It took him a moment to recognize the unfamiliar emotion that gripped him, and then he realized what it was. He felt good. Happy.

"Do you want to walk back or swim?" Aunt Jennifer broke into his thoughts.

"Walk!" David and Laura shouted together. The thought of diving back into the cold water after finally warming up didn't appeal.

Only five families besides Aunt Jennifer summered in Bliss Cove: the Wallaces, who were ancient and spent all their time sitting in beach chairs watching their sailboat bob up and down in the bay, and Matthew's family, the Blooms. Matthew's father worked in Vancouver and came up on the Daddy plane every weekend. Drifter McGee lived by himself year-round in Sand Dollar Bay on the south end of the island. The Smiths and the O'Reillys shared a cove at the northern tip of Fern. Both families had children much younger than the Bliss Cove kids, as the islanders referred to David, Matthew, Laura and Christine.

The days on Fern Island drifted seamlessly into each other, but Fridays were different. Weather permitting, Paul coasted in about three o'clock. He brought with him treats, passengers and news from the mainland. By half past three, he was usually airborne again, with a promise to return Sunday evening to pick up the passengers bound for Vancouver. Sometimes, after a special charter or when there weren't any mainland passengers, Paul would spend the night at Bliss Cove. David loved those times when they'd all have dinner together. Aunt Jennifer would prepare a feast even more delectable than her everyday creations. After dinner the four of them played charades or cribbage or Pictionary. On bright, starlit nights, Paul and Aunt Jennifer, flashlights in hand, would disappear down the path for a late-night trek on the beach. David knew Paul looked forward to those nights when he bunked in with him as much as David did, but he also knew Paul loved his job and didn't mind the pace.

"I'm just an island hopper," he told David. "The people on these islands can set their watches by my arrivals and departures."

Paul kept his promise to David. One Sunday afternoon he flew in an hour earlier. David heard the plane circling from where he sat, buried in a book on the porch. He ran down to the pier.

"Hey, kid," Paul greeted him. "Where's your Auntie?"

"Picking berries with Laura," David replied, disappointed because he'd hoped Paul wanted to see him.

"Perfect, I hoped I'd catch you alone. Let's go for that ride I promised. Don't just stand there with your mouth open. Hop in before everyone in the cove discovers I'm here."

"Really? Shouldn't I leave a note or something for Aunt Jennifer?"

"Your aunt's a pretty smart woman. I think she'll figure it out," Paul said. "Climb on in. You know your way around the cockpit."

They flew at a relatively low altitude, and Paul shared his love of Desolation Sound with David. He knew the names of many of the islands spread below them. Sailboats, powerboats, kayaks and fishing craft large and small dotted the water, some idle in narrow inlets and coves, others moving steadily over the sea, toward destinations Paul and David could only guess. They soared over a luxurious cruise ship headed for Alaska. The people on deck waved up at them from the tennis courts and swimming pool.

David scanned the ocean below, keen to spot more killer whales, but none appeared. Paul's admiration for the great cetaceans was evidenced in his extensive knowledge of their habits and lives. "There are eighty different species of whales and dolphins," he told David. "Did you know that whales are the largest member of the dolphin family?"

David hadn't. Nor had he known that a whale's brain is four times bigger than a human brain. "Although it's no surprise," said Paul. "They're a lot smarter than most humans I know. They're warm-blooded mammals too, just like us."

"So they're top of the food chain?" David asked.

Paul shrugged, never taking his eyes off the expanse of sky and sea. "Sometimes the easiest way to spot whales is to look for a throng of boats." He sighed. "No. Once they *were* top of the food chain, before people discovered them … I think they're the most beautiful creatures on Earth … well, excluding your aunt of course."

David didn't reply, but secretly he was sure Aunt Jennifer thought just as highly of Paul.

As they turned back toward Bliss Cove, David spotted a small island entirely blanketed in trees, just off the north end of Fern. The rocky beach on the west side fell gently toward the water, while steep, granite cliffs rose majestically from the ocean floor on the east side. From the air, the island looked distinctly like a prehistoric animal. "What's the name of that island?" asked David.

"Dragon." Paul replied. "I don't have to explain why."

"Are there any cabins on it?"

"No. The owner lives in Hong Kong. I don't think he's seen it since he bought it. Dragons are good luck for the Chinese," he added.

"It's so close to Fern."

"It's not as close as it looks — nothing is on the ocean — but the currents are legendary in the narrows, especially when the tides are changing. We've got time for a quick flyover if you want." Paul turned his small plane north and they circled Dragon once before returning to Bliss Cove.

The Blooms, along with Aunt Jennifer and Laura, were waiting for them. Paul skidded over the water, and gently butted the Beaver up against the wharf as if nothing in the world was easier. He jumped onto the float and tossed the mooring ropes to Aunt Jennifer and Matthew. "Only one Vancouver-bound?" Paul asked, eyeing Mr. Bloom's overnight bag.

David, to everyone's surprise, popped out of the plane behind Paul.

"No fair!" Laura shouted. "How come he got a ride and I didn't?" Her lower lip shot out in Paul's general direction.

Paul smiled. "Hello to you, too, little miss." He turned to Aunt Jennifer, "And to you." He planted a hasty kiss on her lips.

Aunt Jennifer turned scarlet. "Don't be so cheeky," she scolded, clearly not at all annoyed.

Paul nodded to Mr. Bloom. "Ready? I've got three stops on the way down."

Mr. Bloom hugged his wife, Christine and Matthew. "See you guys next Friday," he said as he climbed into the plane. *I wish I were in their family*, David thought, stunned at his disloyalty.

The Beaver zipped across the water and lifted off, defying gravity. David stood heavily anchored to the ground. In his mind's eye he saw his father holed-up in his small apartment at Yonge and Bloor, the windows closed, the air conditioner at full tilt while he penned another letter to his children. His letters were full of trivia, but each ended in the same way: *Your mother is doing well and sends her love.*

How do you send love? David wondered. *How do you know when it arrives?*

Something Aunt Jennifer had said echoed in his mind. "I can remember many times here on Fern when your mother was so happy." So what had happened?

The last letter from his father had carried disturbing news. He'd written: *I'm considering a trip to the West Coast. If everything works out, I should be able to be with you within the next two to four weeks. I'd like to do some fishing, and dig for clams. I miss you both very much. Your mother is holding her own and sends her love. Love, Dad.*

Dad … on Fern Island. Once, not so long ago, David would have been thrilled, but not now. Now he was happy pretending he had a new family, pretending that his old family didn't exist.

"Earth to David. Come in!" Matthew waved his hand slowly in front of David's face. "David. Where are you?"

"Huh? Sorry." David apologized. "I was thinking about something."

"He's always daydreaming," said Laura to Christine. They giggled and tore off down the wharf, their dolls dangling by their arms.

Aunt Jennifer linked her arm with Matthew's mother. "It's wonderful how those two girls have hit it off." She turned to David. "I was just saying, my friend Eric from Quadra Island has offered to take us salmon fishing. Matthew is invited to come along as well."

"All right!" the boys cried in unison.

"Honey, don't forget I need some clams for tomorrow night. About fifty. You'd better get them now while the tide is low," said Mrs. Bloom.

David liked Matthew's mother. He liked the way she called him "Honey," and Christine, "Sweetie."

"Okay, Mum," sighed Matthew. He picked up the pail that rarely left his side. "Wanna help? Let's go to Sand Dollar Bay. We'll check out Drifter's place. I know he's not in. I saw his old wreck go by a while ago, nobody on it but him. He was dragging a little dinghy behind him. I think he takes it along in case he breaks down out on the water. Everyone says he's crazy mad."

David winced. He hated it when people referred to other people as crazy. "Maybe he's just lonely," he said. "Or maybe he just likes being by himself. Anyway, count me in."

The two boys set off across the island's well-worn footpath. It was a pleasant walk and they'd done it many times before, either on foot or on their bikes. David, always careful to avoid squishing any of the fat green banana slugs that made the forest their home, kept his eyes to the ground.

For a while neither spoke, then Matthew said, "I wanted to work on our raft, not go clamming. You're lucky your mother's far away where she can't bug you and make you do chores."

David didn't feel lucky at all.

There wasn't much to look at in Sand Dollar Bay: an old shack that Drifter called home, a tool shed, a boat shed and a rickety outhouse. An orange buoy anchored out in the sheltered bay waited for Drifter's return. A large, rusty ring screwed into a log on the beach revealed where he secured his dinghy.

They harvested fifty clams together. Matthew showed David how to dig for the clams, keeping only the medium-sized ones for eating. They left the really large ones, which were tough, and the really small ones to thrive in the wet pebbly sand.

"Why are we doing this today, if your mum doesn't need them until tomorrow?" David asked.

"She soaks them overnight," Matthew explained. "It gets the sand out. They spit."

David spat into the water. Matthew followed suit. Pretty soon, the boys collapsed laughing onto the beach, where they stayed until the putt-putt of an outboard roused them.

"Drifter!" shouted Matthew. "Let's get out of here!"

Drifter spotted them from his boat and blew his whistle. "Off my property." He shook his fist at them. "Go on. Get out of here!"

"You're crazy!" Matthew yelled. "A crazy old coot!" He rolled his eyes. "Trespassing. Yeah, right. Nobody owns the beach!"

"Let's get out of here," said David.

The boys fled, lugging the bucket of clams between them. They arrived at Matthew's cabin hot and thirsty.

"What have you two boys been up to?" asked Mrs. Bloom.

"Just clamming. It's hot work," replied Matthew.

"And now we're going swimming," chimed in David.

"Great idea. Tomorrow night, we'll have a clam chowder feast. David, please invite Jennifer and Laura." She peered into the bucket of clams. "Thank you, boys." She smiled kindly.

They spent the rest of the afternoon in and out of the water.

Matthew showed David how to ride drifting logs as if they were wild horses. Laura and Christine joined in. Laura, fearless as always, seemed unperturbed by the long, slimy bull kelp that hovered near the shore, but David wouldn't venture in without his water shoes on, a fact he guarded carefully.

Matthew kept the other three tearing in and out of the water by yelling "Dog!" every time he spotted the shadow of dogfish gliding near them, and often when he didn't.

"Those poor dogfish have gotten a bad rap," Aunt Jennifer told them over dinner that night. "They're just trying to survive, like everything else in the ocean. I've eaten one, you know. You probably have, too, in fish and chips. The fishermen don't like them because they eat their bait right off the hook. If they catch a dogfish, they throw it back, or more likely they kill it, but they don't die easily."

Every evening, David and Laura listened to Aunt Jennifer's stories about Fern Island and Desolation Sound. They learned about the early loggers, fishermen and pilots who had settled in Desolation Sound and the Native people who'd been there before them. David loved stories about Jim Spilsbury, the founder of Queen Charlotte Airlines — QCA — a bush outfit that grew into Canada's third largest airline. The locals jokingly called it "Queer Collection of Aircraft." Jim Spilsbury had spent his school-age years on nearby Savary Island long before it was a tourist destination.

Aunt Jennifer believed that living in Desolation Sound, or visiting it, carried a large responsibility. "We are stewards of the land," she said. "We're never alone here. Life is everywhere and it's up to us to look after it."

Sometimes late at night, when the bunkhouse lay in darkness and the fire crackled, David thought about his mother and father. He knew Laura did, too, because on those nights he would hear her tossing and turning and eventually she would climb into the empty bunk in his room.

Mostly he thought about his mother, and it worried him that he could no longer picture her face clearly. When that happened, he would take out her photo and stare at it. Maybe she was getting better, now that he and Laura weren't around to bother her.

The letters from their father continued to arrive and David stubbornly continued not to write back. His father wrote of his plans to visit Fern Island, and as the day drew nearer and nearer, David grew less and less comfortable with the idea of his pending visit.

Aunt Jennifer had delayed the fishing trip with Eric. "I think it'll be something your father might enjoy, too," she said. "I'm sure he'd like to try his hand at salmon fishing."

Aunt Jennifer, David suspected, was as nervous about the visit as he was, but true to her nature she'd decided not to worry over things she couldn't change. So the days flowed into each other, and before anyone realized it July turned into August. Their father would be arriving on the Daddy plane the following Friday.

Laura seemed genuinely excited. This infuriated David, and he slowly began to withdraw into his own world. At night, instead of sitting around the fireplace and talking to Aunt Jennifer, he buried himself in books about orcas, and sketched their majestic black and white bodies on sheets of paper. He felt a strong affinity with the huge creatures — perhaps because they too lived in a world just outside of their control.

Chapter Seven

DAVID was late. He found Matthew in his favourite place: at the wharf, jigging for cod. He looked lazily up at David. "What took you so long? I thought you'd be here earlier?"

"Wood day," David replied shortly. Lately a lot of stuff bothered David, including that Matthew did not have to do chores, unless you counted digging for clams a chore.

"What about yesterday? You didn't even show up." Matthew moved his rod up and down in the waves absently. "I thought we were supposed to collect moon snail shells."

"Couldn't make it," David said tersely. "Did you find any?"

"Yeah." Matthew dug into his pocket and extracted a creamy white shell a moon snail had abandoned.

David whistled. It was easily the size of his fist, but he knew that the animal that until recently had occupied the shell might be two or three times larger. Aunt Jennifer had explained that it often could not fit its entire body into the shell. The boys had come across plenty of evidence of the moon snail on Fern Island. The snails laid their eggs in perfectly symmetrical circles on the sand, and hunted down their prey at literally a "snail's pace," chasing down the even slower clams and other snails.

David was as fascinated with moon snails as he had been with spiders. He studied the empty shell carefully and tried to imagine the animal that had once occupied it. Like a spider, it would be both beautiful and cruel. He remembered his aunt's words: "The moon snail wraps its prey in its large foot to immobilize it, then drills through the shell to the meaty inside. It might take three minutes, or days. Sometimes moon snails drill two or three holes to get to their main course. That's why some of the clam shells you'll find have more than one hole."

It seemed a slow and agonizing death, comparable to a fly cocooned in a spider's web.

"Wow," said David, his black mood momentarily suspended. "It's a nice one. Can I have it?"

Matthew shoved it back into his pocket. "Give me a break," he said.

David sat down beside his friend, too dejected to bother with his own fishing gear. Since the news of his father's confirmed arrival, he'd lost interest in the things he liked to do on the island. "My dad's flying in with your dad this Friday," he said.

"Is your mother coming, too?"

How to explain that his mother and father didn't even live together?

If Matthew noticed David's non-answer, he didn't let on. "Aren't you excited to see him? I mean, I don't think I've ever been away from my dad for more than two weeks."

Half of David was thrilled; the other half didn't care if he never saw his father again. He shrugged, turning his attention to an eagle intent on his own fishing expedition. It let out a piercing screech before diving toward the sea, talons out, ready to pierce the soft flesh of the unlucky salmon it had spotted from the sky. Eagles, David knew, mated for life. The boys watched the great bird pluck its prey from the water and fly off toward the craggy tree they'd identified as its home.

"Aunt Jennifer says to remind you that next Saturday we're going fishing with her friend Eric."

"I know Eric," replied Matthew. "As if I'd forget …"

◑

Friday arrived on a flaming red sky. After lunch, David stood on the porch and scanned the flat calm water. Soon his father would be here. He sniffed the air, the way he'd seen Aunt Jennifer do so many times over the past six weeks.

"It smells like a storm," he said to her.

Aunt Jennifer inhaled deeply as if she could taste the weather. "I think you're right. We're in for some wind and rain." She licked her index finger and held it high above her head. Laura did the same.

"What the heck," David said and moistened his own finger. The air brushed his damp skin, rich with information.

"Southwesterly, definitely in for some foul weather," said Aunt Jennifer. "I hope Paul will be able to land this afternoon."

"The ocean looks like a mirror, though," said David. "Maybe your finger's wrong?"

"Maybe, but not likely. Did you see the sunrise this morning?"

David remembered the blood-red sky. The eagles had woken him, calling to each other, exchanging information about the fattest fish, and David had opened his eyes to a horizon on fire.

"I'll bet your mother used to recite this little rhyme to you two:

> Red sky at night,
> Sailors' delight.
> Red sky at morning,
> Sailors take warning."

"She did!" shouted Laura. "She did all the time."

David shifted his body into a close imitation of their aunt — hand on hips, chin thrust out and eyes wide. "Nature talks to you, if only you know her language."

"You monkey." Aunt Jennifer tousled his hair. "I don't sound like that!"

"You do," David laughed.

She smiled at him, her soft green eyes pleased. "Well, anyway, you're learning fast."

"Let's eat. I'm starved again!" Laura tugged on her aunt's sleeve. David smiled. Laura didn't depend on him the way she used to, and he knew he had his aunt to thank for that.

"Nothing like the outdoors to work up an appetite," said Aunt Jennifer, "and I'll bet David could use a snack, too. I've been baking since sunrise. Follow your noses." She opened the screen door and they all crowded into the kitchen where a fresh batch of cinnamon buns sat cooling on the counter.

"I hope Dad brings me a letter from Bill," David said. He closed his eyes and revelled in the explosion of sugar and berries in his mouth. He reached for another bun. "These are delicious. Before Fern Island, I'd never heard of blackberry cinnamon buns."

Aunt Jennifer raised her eyebrows and grinned. "I don't hear any complaints."

Blackberries grew wild all over the island, but harvesting them went side by side with scratches and scrapes. David, Laura and Aunt Jennifer had set out early yesterday morning and returned an hour later lugging a bucket full to the brim with sweet, juicy berries. David looked at his sister and aunt — their mouths stained a deep purple. He laughed and they joined in.

"I hope Dad brings me presents," said Laura between bites. "Lots of presents!"

"I hope the weather doesn't get so bad he can't land," David said, although he thought the opposite, in spite of the jokes and banter.

Aunt Jennifer licked her sticky fingers. She stared longingly at the plate of gooey buns.

"We'll see. It may blow over yet. You know how unpredictable the weather is up here." She sighed. "If I eat one more bun, I'll put on another whole pound!"

Unlikely, David thought. His aunt's appetite was eclipsed only by her energy.

"You're so different from Mum," he said, unconsciously dropping his guard. "She doesn't like to bake, or eat for that matter. She just stays in her room, or wanders around the house in her nightgown … at least now." He stopped — he hadn't meant to criticize. "She reads a lot," he added, "at least she used to."

"She wasn't always the way she is now, David," Aunt Jennifer said sadly. "For as long as I can remember she used to love fishing, boating and swimming. When you were young, her greatest pleasure was being with you." She smiled across the table at Laura. "She was so proud when you were born."

"What happened?" Laura asked simply. "What did we do?"

Aunt Jennifer frowned. "Nothing. You did nothing at all. Your mother's depression isn't anyone's fault, not even her own. About five years ago, your dad started to notice that she didn't seem herself. He phoned me, and I suggested you all come out to Vancouver for Christmas. Do you remember?"

David and Laura nodded slowly.

"Well," Aunt Jennifer continued, "I could see something was wrong. I tried to talk to her, but she insisted it was only a rough period in her life. She said she just felt tired. I didn't pursue it with her." She sighed, absently reaching for another cinnamon bun. "That's my regret, that I did nothing for her back then. You see, she was still coping, and your dad and I both put it down to her feeling a little overwhelmed. It got worse, and we didn't really notice until it was too late." She placed her strong, rough hand on David's. "You've had to grow up awfully fast."

David pulled his hand away. "I'm supposed to go fishing with Matthew." He pushed back his chair and it crashed to the floor. "Sorry. See you later."

"Wait, David." Aunt Jennifer picked his chair up off the floor.

David stood, legs apart, arms crossed, a scowl on his face. "What? Are you going to tell me everything's going to be fine? Or are you going to tell me I should just be patient and that time will heal everything?" He swallowed quickly. "Or maybe you want us to know that it's okay that Dad walked out on us?"

"I know it's been a tough haul …"

"No! No, you don't know!" David shouted, suddenly unable to control his anger. "Don't try to pretend you know what it's been like. Nobody knows."

Laura began to cry.

"Why don't you stop snivelling?" David snapped. "Do you think Mum liked listening to you whine and cry all the time?"

"I hate you!" screamed Laura.

"Well, finally," said Aunt Jennifer. "A little bit of honesty from the both of you. Sit down, David." She wrapped her arms around Laura. "Have yourself a good cry."

David dropped into his chair and rested his head on the table. Honesty — a sentiment that, over the years, had become less and less valued in the Garrett family. He stayed like that, still and thoughtful, until Laura's tears subsided, and his own sense of anger and loss also abated. Aunt Jennifer did not hurry them, but when David raised his head, she continued, without any of the awkward references or sympathetic clicks so second nature to most grown-ups.

"Next Friday we go salmon fishing. Look forward to that. I am. The downside is we'll have to get up at five-thirty ..." She cocked her head to one side. "Listen."

They all heard it — the distant throb of a seaplane. David glanced at his watch. "If it's Paul, he's early."

"He's decided to get in and out before the storm hits. Go on ahead, David. Laura and I will grab a tissue and be right behind you."

David rushed out the door and into the dreary prestorm light. He hit the path at a full run and broke out of the trees at the same time as the first big raindrops began to pummel the beach.

Paul had managed to bring the pontoons onto the water, but the little Beaver pitched and reared as she plowed through the chop toward the wharf. Already a group of islanders, including Matthew and his family, had gathered there and David joined them. In true island spirit, most of the inhabitants had turned out ready to lend a hand to Paul if he needed it.

It looked as if he might. He guided the small plane in and cut the engines at the last moment. Phil O'Reilly and Matthew's mother stood ready to receive the bow and stern lines.

"Pull her in and hold her fast!" shouted Paul, emerging onto the pontoon. He fought to be heard above the wind and waves and rain. "I have to get out of here in a hurry!"

David helped Mrs. Bloom and they struggled to steady the plane. The wet rope burned their hands, but they held on. The rain drove into them.

A sudden gust of wind slammed into the Beaver and her pontoon bashed against the wharf.

"Keep her steady and off the wood!" yelled Paul. He braced himself against the wing for support. "Try to push her nose in so she's facing into the wind."

He'd hardly spoken when the wind gusted in another direction.

"A bit of a squall!" shouted Aunt Jennifer. "Bumpy ride in?"

Paul grinned and nodded. "Nothing the Beaver can't handle, but the passengers — some of them are a little green around the gills." He unlatched the cabin door. "Everybody out. Loosen up the bow line, now. I want her nose out. They can deplane on the stern."

On cue, a smallish foot emerged out of the cabin door. A small-ish foot clad in sparkling new, white running shoes. It settled tentatively on the top foothold. Paul reached up to offer his hand. "Move along. Nothing to be afraid of. You're almost on land," he coaxed.

A large roller glanced off the nose of the little plane. She swung sideways, then another wave hit the Beaver broadside, sending her careening into the wharf. "Hold her fast!" Paul yelled, almost los-ing his footing. And then everything happened at once.

The wearer of the new white running shoes tumbled out of the seaplane and slid gracefully onto the pontoon. She balanced there for a split second, her eyes wide open, then she fell into the choppy sea. Aunt Jennifer, clear-headed, lunged toward the life-saving ring that hung permanently on the wharf. Laura screamed, and Mrs. Bloom and David both dropped the Beaver's bow line. Her nose bucked and drifted away from the wharf, until she pointed directly out to sea.

"Damn it! Don't let go of the stern line!" yelled Paul.

For David, everything unfolded in slow motion. For a brief and joyful second, he'd imagined that perhaps the woman in the new, white runners might be his mother. When he realized who it was, a wave of disappointment paralyzed him. *Serves her right*, he thought.

Aunt Jennifer hurled the life-saving ring toward the woman flailing in the water. "Catch this!" she called. To no one in particular, she said, "Who is that?"

While Aunt Jennifer sprang into action, Paul, a grim look on his normally relaxed face, retrieved the bow line, leapt off the pontoon and landed with a thud on the wharf. He guided the Beaver's nose away from the figure in the water.

"Have you got her, Jenn?" he called urgently.

"Under control," Aunt Jennifer replied, a little too gleefully.

Paul shook his head. He smiled, leaned over and gave her a peck on the cheek. "Thanks. You're beautiful."

A large man dressed in grey trousers and a blue jacket poked his head out the cabin door. Behind him, another man peered out, a worried expression on his round face.

"Dad!" cried Matthew and David in unison.

"That's my dad," David said to Matthew.

"Duh," Matthew replied.

"Daddy!" Laura squealed.

Aunt Jennifer pulled the reluctant swimmer from the water. "Wrap yourself in this," she instructed, pulling off her sweater and handing it to the trembling woman, who stood shivering in the chilly wind.

She took the sweater, removed her own sopping jacket and pulled it over her head. "Thanks. The water's freezing. What a botch-up," she added.

David stared. It couldn't be! Dad wouldn't do this! He took a step backward, almost losing his footing, and tried to collect his thoughts. Kathleen!

"It's not that cold," he said.

She smiled at him, her teeth chattering. "Hello everyone."

David watched his father and Mr. Bloom deplane. How could he bring her here?

"David! How's my boy?" The words scattered, and unintelligible, blew over David like the wind. He blinked.

"Boys." Paul caught his eye. "Give me a hand with the luggage." He pulled three large suitcases and an overnight bag out of the storage compartment in the pontoon and passed them across to Matthew and David.

"See you Sunday!" he called to Aunt Jennifer, his eyebrows raised in an unspoken question.

"Who's the not-so-sure-footed lady?" Matthew whispered to David. "Is that your mother?"

"God, no!" David struggled for words. "That's Kathleen, my dad's girlfriend."

"You're kidding! I didn't know your mum and dad were divorced."

"They're not. They're separated."

The plane rumbled to life and taxied over the foaming water.

"Well, anyway, Laura seems to like her." He nodded his head to where Laura stood, her arms wrapped around Kathleen.

"Laura likes anyone who pays attention to her." David rolled his eyes. "Except insects," he added.

Aunt Jennifer turned to David's father. "Is this supposed to be your surprise, John?" Mr. Garrett stood frozen like a deer caught in the headlights of a car. "I hope not," continued Aunt Jennifer. "I hope you've come alone."

He ignored his sister-in-law, turning instead to David, but was stopped by the smouldering anger evident in his eyes.

Laura intervened. "Daddy!" She left Kathleen's side and jumped into her father's arms. He scooped her up, and planted a big kiss on her cheek. "How's my little girl? Am I ever glad to see you! Where's that doll of yours?"

David fixed his eyes on the Beaver, now a speck in the dark sky.

"She's napping," replied Laura.

"And Mum?" said David. "How's Mum?"

"Okay, everyone," Aunt Jennifer interrupted. "Let's get your friend up to the cabin and into some warm clothes. Laura, show her the way. We'll follow with the luggage."

Everyone stepped back to allow Kathleen and Laura to pass through the uncomfortable silence. Finally Mr. Bloom spoke.

"We're off, too." he said. "Nice chatting with you on the way up, John."

"What did you talk about on the flight up?" David scowled. "Our crazy family? My dad's new girlfriend?"

"David," Aunt Jennifer said shortly. "Help me with this stuff." She smiled briefly at Matthew's father. "I'm sorry," she said. "All this is rather … unexpected." She waved her arms hopelessly.

"Don't apologize for me," David spat. "Apologize for him." He glared once more at his father. "I'm outta here." David bolted up the ramp and tore down the pier. By the time he reached the beach, he couldn't tell if he was blinded by the fierce rain or his tears.

The sky was now an ominous black. A clap of thunder boomed overhead. David looked out to sea and counted slowly to five. Another one, louder this time, echoed around him. The electrified air slapped against his cold, wet skin. Still he stayed on the beach. The midsummer storm raged around him.

Chapter Eight

THAT week might have been the worst in David's life. Might have been but wasn't, thanks to Aunt Jennifer. She managed to keep them all more or less busy and apart. David and his father had hardly spoken, but David hadn't been unhappy, not all the time. He'd spent his days with Matthew and become much better at operating Aunt Jennifer's aluminum boat. They'd set crab traps, swum, built a fort on the beach and sometimes just found private places to read or talk.

Finally, the Thursday before their fishing trip arrived. That night before dinner, David was grateful when Aunt Jennifer suggested a bout of wood-cutting. He was even more grateful when she paved the way for him to slip into the bunkhouse immediately after they'd eaten.

"Early to bed," she said. "Eric will be at the wharf at five-thirty tomorrow morning."

This dinner, like the others, had been tension-filled. Aunt Jennifer addressed Kathleen in a cool and removed manner. David had said little, except for demanding news of his mother.

"Why didn't you bring her here?" he asked his father, not for the first time. "Aunt Jennifer says she was always happy here on Fern Island."

"I don't think she's up to the long journey." His father sounded edgy.

"Did you ask her?" David got up and took their family photo down from the mantelpiece. Deliberately he set it down in front of Kathleen. "See, that's what my mother looks like when she's happy," he said. "She'd be happy here."

Kathleen, to David's satisfaction, looked decidedly uncomfortable. "I know it must be terribly difficult …" she began.

Aunt Jennifer shot her a dark look, putting an abrupt stop to the conversation. "Would anyone else like to come fishing with us in the morning?" she asked.

Laura, as usual, seemed unperturbed. "I'll do whatever Daddy does," she said, happily. David kicked her under the table. Didn't she get it?

"Ouch!" she yelped.

Kathleen got it. She turned to David. "I think I've had enough of the water," she said in a lame attempt at humour. "I'd prefer to stay on dry land. I'm sure you won't mind?"

Mind? "Sure. Whatever," David mumbled.

"Okay." His father rubbed his forehead absently. "I'd like to go fishing," he said. "I really would — but …" He avoided David's eyes, smiling instead at Laura and Kathleen. "But tomorrow I think I'll stay here with my girls."

David didn't know if he felt disappointed or elated. Even if he hadn't been as welcoming as Laura, big suck that she was, he'd assumed that his father would want to go on the fishing trip.

"Speaking of *your girls,*" he said, "how's Mum, really?" David pushed back his chair and stood abruptly. "Don't bother telling us. You've already made it pretty clear."

"Not to me," piped up Laura. "I want to know how Mum is. I really miss her." She put down her fork. "Is she going to get better soon?"

Kathleen cleared her throat. Aunt Jennifer stared at David's father, while David waited poised for flight.

"Your mother is on a new medication." He sighed. "The other drugs had side effects that didn't agree with her. She seems a little better, but the doctors, well, they say it's a bit of a waiting game." He sounded discouraged. "She's up and out of bed every day now, and she's shown a real interest in her garden again. We have to be patient. This new medication should help her cope."

Laura tilted her head. "What's cope?"

"Right now your mother feels very sad and overwhelmed by everything. That's why she has no energy."

"By us." Laura's lower lip stuck out. "You mean by us. Don't you? David and me. She's better 'cause we're away."

"I'm going to bed," said David. He couldn't bear to hear any more. He closed the door, thankful that his father and Kathleen would be bunking on the hide-a-bed couch in the main house. At least he'd have privacy.

In the bunkhouse he lit the fire, then climbed into bed even though it was only nine o'clock. It took him a long time to fall asleep. The past week had brought back a flood of conflicting emotions. He missed his mother so much he could pinpoint the ache in the pit of his belly. But it was the mother of the past that he longed for — the shiny-eyed, alert, fun adult who'd made him feel that he was the only person in the whole world who truly mattered.

The sun had long set when David drifted into a fitful sleep. Aunt Jennifer woke him as dawn broke, and they crept out of the cabin into a clear summer morning. Matthew waited for them on the wharf. Eric, too, comfortable with a cup of coffee in the back of his trawler, *The Theodosia*. It was an old boat, similar to Drifter McGee's *Corky*, but in better repair. "I spend all my spare time on her," Eric explained, rubbing the wooden gunwale lovingly. "Has everyone got their licences?"

They did. David and Aunt Jennifer had bought fishing licences the previous week in Lund.

They set out on a flat sea, the sun casting prisms across the water's surface. Yesterday's wind, strong and constant, had died and there wasn't a cloud in the sky. David planted himself in the stern and watched Bliss Cove fade into the distance. "I know you wanted your dad to come fishing today," Aunt Jennifer began. "I don't want to make excuses for him, but …"

"Then don't." David moved forward to where Eric and Matthew stood mesmerized in front of the beeping fish finder.

It resembled a small TV screen, but instead of showing programs, it scanned the sea below for movement. "That big cloud on the screen is probably a school of herring," Eric told them, "and that means there should be salmon close behind."

They powered north for an hour, meandering among the small islands dotting Desolation Sound. Eric helped the boys set up their rods. "I'll do it once," he said, "but after that you look after your own gear." David watched, feeling slightly queasy as Eric netted a live herring from his bait tank, and impaled it on the hook, double-checking to make sure it couldn't squirm its way to freedom. Then he attached the rods to the downriggers, so the hooks would sink into the deep ocean. "Watch your lines for movement," he advised. "First the fish will bite, then he'll run. When that happens, play out your line. The idea is to tire the big guy out before trying to haul him in. Jennifer's a pro."

David got the first bite. He played the fish under Eric's watchful eye for twenty minutes. Three times it almost got away, but at last they managed to haul it to the gunwales. Matthew wielded an awkward telescoping net. He leaned far out over the side of the boat, struggling to place it beneath the thrashing salmon. After several attempts he was able to bring it aboard.

"A coho, at least six kilos!" exclaimed Eric, thumping David on the back. "Nice size for your first ever fish. Finish him off." He handed David a short baseball bat. "Whack him hard so you only have to do it once."

At his feet, the salmon, *his* salmon, gulped in gillfulls of poisonous air, in a fight for his life. A small pool of crimson blood spread beneath his magnificent silver body. Brilliant red blood spotted the deck. The large, three-pronged hook protruded menacingly out of the side of its convulsing mouth. A bead of perspiration rolled down David's forehead and into his eye. He'd never killed anything in his life, discounting the wood bugs he'd collected for his spider.

"Put it out of its misery," encouraged Aunt Jennifer gently.

David raised the bat high, then stopped. An urgent voice inside his head seemed to plead with him not to strike.

"What a beauty," said Matthew. "Want me to kill it?"

David brought the bat down heavily just above the gills, as Eric had told him. The fish stopped thrashing and lay still in its own blood. David stared down at it, feeling a mixture of pride and regret. "That's a big fish," he said.

"Way to go, David," said Eric.

David smiled. His arms ached and his T-shirt stuck to his back. "Let's have a picture," said Aunt Jennifer, brandishing her camera. "Your mother will be thrilled." David hoisted his catch and grinned into the lens. The fish glistened in the sun, its body rainbow-coloured. "We'll clean it when we get back to Bliss Cove. It'll make a fine feast." Aunt Jennifer licked her lips. "My mouth is watering at the thought of it."

Eric wasn't a big talker, but he had plenty to say about the salmon fishery. "When I was about your age," he told the boys, "my dad and I fished this area all the time. All you had to do was drop your line in the water and you were guaranteed a fish. No downriggers, no fish finders or other fancy equipment. Good eating fish too: salmon, halibut, rock cod. No dogfish, at least not too often." He pointed off the port side of the boat. "Look who's here! There's competition!"

A large brown-eyed sea lion dove under the boat and sur-faced on the starboard side. "Thank your lucky stars he wasn't here when you were reeling in your fish. He'd have stolen it off your hook before you could blink!" The sea lion peered at them expectantly. "He's after scraps," said Eric, chuckling. "A real oppor-tunist. Some fishermen shoot them," he added sadly. "It's illegal, but out here, who's to stop them?"

David stared at the massive sea lion, which eyed him back fear-lessly. "How could anyone hurt you?" he wondered aloud.

"Too many predators and not enough prey," said Aunt Jennifer.

David looked at her, puzzled. "What?"

"Too many fishermen, and not enough fish," explained Eric. "And we all blame each other. The commercial fishery blames the Native fishery, the sports fishers blame the commercial and the Native fisheries. Some people blame the fish farms, and oth-ers blame pollution, and on and on. Meanwhile, the fish stocks keep depleting, while we argue about whose fault it is."

"Well, everyone should just stop fishing, then," said Matthew.

"Tell that to a guy who has to feed his family and maintain his boat, a guy who doesn't know any other way of life." He paused. "A guy like me. Life is just not that simple."

"Everyone wants the same thing," interjected Aunt Jennifer. "A sustainable fishery. Hopefully we've learned our lesson from the East Coast fishery disasters. Still, it's a long process, and people usually only think of their own interests."

"Not us," said Eric lashing David's rod securely to the side of the boat. "One fish per person. After lunch we'll concentrate on Matthew."

Aunt Jennifer was in charge of lunch and it was scrumptious. Tuna sandwiches, blackberry buns, lemonade, and barbecue chips, followed by chocolate bars all around.

A couple of hours later, Matthew reeled in a four kilo coho, but not until he'd lost three other good-sized fish off his line. This time it was David's turn to wield the net, struggling to scoop it under the panicked fish without tangling the line.

By half past three, Aunt Jennifer announced, "nap time." Eric stored the day's catch in the bait tanks, and anchored the boat in a protected cove. The two adults stretched out on the deck, pulled their hats down over their eyes and promptly fell asleep.

David and Matthew perched on the gunwales, dipping their feet into the steel-blue sea. The hot sun beat down on them as it advanced slowly over the water. David felt relaxed for the first time since his father had arrived.

"Listen to your aunt," Matthew laughed. "She's snoring!"

David grinned. "I know. I can hear her through the walls at night, and we don't even sleep in the same cabin."

"David, I'm ... I'm sorry about your dad showing up with his ... with that lady, Kathleen. And I'm sorry about your mother. My mum knows her, and she really likes her. If there's anything ... I mean, I know it must be hard with your mum and all ..." Matthew paused and shifted uncomfortably. David sat silently, gazing up at the old trees crowded together on the rocky shore. "What I'm trying to say is ..."

The high, long squeal of an eagle finished Matthew's sentence.

"There she is!" He pointed to the sky, where the majestic bird soared overhead, riding invisible air currents. David sensed Matthew's discomfort. He hadn't known him very long, and he'd never allowed anyone, not even Bill, to discuss the turmoil that raged inside of him. Yet somehow, today, it felt all right to talk.

"I just want everything to be normal, like it is in your family," he said, never taking his eyes off the eagle.

"Yeah," agreed Matthew.

"But I guess Eric is right. Things can't always be that simple."

"Yeah, I guess," Matthew answered.

"Anyway, thanks." David pulled off his shirt. "What about a swim before it's time to go back?"

Matthew didn't bother to strip down. He leapt off the boat into the ocean. A seal popped up beside him. "Arf," Matthew barked at it. "Arf! Arf!"

David, less fearful now of the abundant sea life in Desolation Sound, jumped in beside him, barking and splashing. The seal, startled but still curious, bumped up against his leg before diving out of sight. The boys followed suit, wiggling their bodies through the water in pursuit of the animal.

Eric and Aunt Jennifer, drawn out of sleep by the laughing and splashing, took pictures of the strange playmates. "I've never seen that before," said Eric. "It's just a young seal, not old enough to have much fear."

"Can we take him home with us?" David joked.

"I don't think so," Aunt Jennifer laughed. "Even if we could, he — or she — must have a mother around somewhere."

The seal, as if agreeing, barked once more and disappeared under the water. David and Matthew, cold now, climbed on board and Eric turned the boat toward Bliss Cove. By the time they arrived on Fern, the sun hung above the mountains of Vancouver Island to the west.

The boys gutted and cleaned their salmon on the wharf, while Eric supervised. It was a messy job, one that the seagulls delighted in, hovering overhead hoping for a tasty morsel of fish entrails. Eric's knife slashed through the belly of the salmon easily, spilling guts onto the wooden planks. "Do you want fillets or steaks for dinner?" Aunt Jennifer asked.

"Steak for me," said David.

"Ditto," said Matthew.

They tossed the fish heads and tails to the squawking gulls. "Greedy birds," Aunt Jennifer laughed, watching them battle until not a scrap remained. She tried to convince Eric to stay for the salmon feast, but his own family waited for him.

"Thanks!" David and Matthew called. They watched until Eric's boat had turned the point, then gathered up their steaks.

"Thanks for taking me fishing today," Matthew said to Aunt Jennifer. "It was great. Mum'll be happy I've brought dinner! See you tomorrow David."

"See ya. And Matthew, thanks. For everything."

The thick salmon steaks tasted like summer. They ate outdoors in the soft evening light, something they could never have done in Muskoka, where the bugs would have made a meal of the humans. Here, the only really annoying insect was the wasp. Aunt Jennifer set up her wasp trap.

"There's nothing those yellow-jackets like more than fresh-caught salmon," she explained.

It was true. They came from nowhere, drawn by the sweet, heavy aroma of barbecued salmon.

"Try to ignore them," said their father to Kathleen.

"How? They're on my food."

Aunt Jennifer swatted at them lazily. "They have great taste," she laughed. "Who can blame them?"

"Well, I don't like them," complained Laura. "I'm going to eat inside."

Kathleen smiled at her. "I think I'll join you. Delicious salmon, David. Thank you." She didn't wait for him to reply, which was just as well, because he didn't plan to. Over the past week, Kathleen and David had reached an uneasy truce — David ignored all of her overtures and Kathleen stayed out of his way as much as possible.

When they were gone, David's father said, "Tell me about your day fishing."

David took a long slurp of milk, put down his knife and fork and stood up. "I hate her," he said. "You might not think it's fair, but I hate her."

David's father flushed crossly and started to speak. David held up his hand. "Wait. I'm not finished. You should never have come here, at least not with your stupid girlfriend. What about my mother?" Hot tears welled up in his eyes, and he swiped them away angrily. "It's not just our fault she's depressed and sad. You made her the way she is!"

"David, that's not true! It's nobody's fault. Not mine, not Laura's, not hers and certainly not yours. She's ill. Clinically depressed." A small groan escaped his father. "I couldn't live that way any-more." He leaned forward and let his head droop. "I just couldn't take it anymore, and neither could you and your sister."

"Nobody ever asked us!" David screamed. "Nobody!" He turned and ran.

"Let him go," he heard his aunt say. "He needs to be alone." David ran down the dark path, back to the beach, throwing himself on the warm sand. The beach was deserted. He lay on his back listening to the waves rolling gently, and watched the full yellow moon sink lower and lower on the horizon. Nothing mattered. He didn't care that it was cold, he didn't care if anyone heard his sobs. David lay there until the weight of his sadness lifted a little, then he stood up and trudged slowly back to the bunkhouse.

Chapter Nine

"**D**AVID!** David! Are you awake? I can't go back to sleep. I didn't know if you'd come back earlier." Laura was shaking his shoulder.

David rolled over sleepily and pulled the duvet up around his chin. By the time he'd crept back to the bunkhouse, the cabin had lain in darkness, but an idea had begun to materialize.

"David, I'm freezing standing here. Can I sleep in the top bunk? I had a bad dream. An awake bad dream."

He groaned and snuggled more deeply into his covers. "I don't care where you sleep, just leave me alone." He burrowed his chin deeper into his pillow and chased his own dream, but it was too late. The hot Muskoka rocks were gone. The heavy, humid air, the tepid lake water … all gone.

"I know you were mad at dinner," Laura whispered. "You miss Mum. I miss her too," she added in a choked voice. "I knew she was sad, but I never asked her why. I thought it would go away if I was really good and did what I was told."

David opened his eyes and stared into the darkness. Images of last summer when his family had been intact crowded him. "Remember last July and August at the lake?" he said. "Every Thursday, Dad would drive up for the weekend."

"Mmm. Tell me more," Laura said.

David thought about Bliss Cove, where dads fall out of the

sky in Daddy planes and are taken away on wings on Sunday nights. "He always brought us something from Toronto. Candy, or Bill or …"

"Relief," interrupted Laura.

"Relief?"

Laura mimicked their mother perfectly, even remembering to sigh heavily before she began to speak in a defeated voice. *"I can't wait for your father to get here, so I can have some relief."*

"I guess at some point he ran out of that," David said, remembering that she'd cried a lot in those months. "I asked her what was wrong," he said, sitting up, "but she never told me."

"Aunt Jennifer and Daddy argued for a long time after you left the table tonight," said Laura. "They were yelling at each other, and they made me go for a walk with Kathleen. That's why I woke up. I think they're at it again. I heard them on the deck a minute ago."

"Just now?" David asked, fully awake.

"Just before I came in here. Everything was fine until Daddy came. I wish they'd both go home." Her voice quavered.

David sat up. "Are they still out there?"

"I think so. They thought I was asleep. Aunt Jennifer even came in and checked, but I wasn't, not really. You were," she added accusingly, wiping away a tear with her fist.

David groped around in the dark, located his sweatshirt, and pulled it over his head. "I have to hear what they're saying. You stay here with Susie, and don't worry. I'll be right back." He slipped out of bed into the shadows.

Silently, he tiptoed across the floor and opened the door carefully. The moon hung in a glorious disc against the black sky and shafts of light speared the porch, illuminating Aunt Jennifer and John Garrett huddled together at the table, a solitary candle flickering between them. He slipped noiselessly into a pocket of darkness beneath the arbutus tree, straining to hear their conversation.

"What would you have me tell them?" his father anguished.

"The truth," Aunt Jennifer replied. "They're smart kids — they can handle the truth more easily than they can half-lies."

"I don't even know what the truth is anymore." His father's body seemed to shrink into the chair. He rubbed his temples before lifting his eyes to the night sky. "Jennifer, you've got to believe me when I say I've tried. I've tried for years, but I can't take it anymore. She just gets worse and worse. Maybe if I'd paid more attention to her mood swings in the beginning, but that's all I thought they were — mood swings. The drugs help, a little, but she still cries a lot. I can't talk to her. No one can. You haven't been around her lately." He looked at his sister-in-law as if pleading for understanding or forgiveness or maybe both.

"You should have told me how bad it was. You moved out, left her alone with the kids and didn't even call. I could have helped. I'm her sister, John. It's taken almost a month for David to start behaving like a kid again and as long for Laura to stop treating him like a parent. I won't let you take them back to all that, and to a new girlfriend. Leave them here until the end of summer, and then we'll make some decisions. I can't believe how selfish you're being," she added.

Exasperated, his father replied, "I'm not going to take them back to all that. It will be different. It has to be … They can stay with me and I can get someone in to help with the kids. They need to come home."

David wiggled uncomfortably in his hiding place pushed up against the soft bark of the arbutus. Nothing they said shocked him, but their words made it all so real. The hurt surprised him.

"It's my decision," said his father firmly. "They're my children, not yours. Besides, Kathleen is right. They need to get to know her, to accept her, and they can't do it here, where they run wild every day. Please, I want you on side, but I am taking them back to Toronto, whether you approve or not."

"Oh. I see." Aunt Jennifer stood up, her eyes blazing. "You're right, they're not my children, but they're my sister's children and I love them. Their mother is sick, and you think they should just live with that, forget about it and accept Kathleen! I suppose you expect them to be thrilled to get a new mother. The old one is crazy, but the new model is perfectly sane. Try her out, you might like her better!"

David recoiled at her anger, and at the truth she spoke. His father's fist crashed down on the table, upending the candle and sending it toppling to the deck, where it extinguished.

"Damn it, Jennifer, you have a way of twisting everything around so the good looks bad. At least Kathleen isn't walking around in a trance, crying all her waking hours away. At least she would eat dinner with us at night, and get out of bed in the morning." He retrieved the candle and plonked it back down on the table. "At least she'll talk to us," he declared sadly.

Aunt Jennifer shook her head vigorously. "I understand all that, but it's too early. David and Laura need to realize that their mother has a long road ahead of her. They need to have the time to deal with that before they can accept someone else in their lives. John, it's the wrong way to go about it. I beg you, leave them here for the rest of the summer, let them get used to the idea." She reached over and placed her hand on top of his. "Please, John. I know we can work something out."

He abruptly pulled his hand away. "No, Jenn. I don't want to wait any longer. In two days, when the plane leaves, we'll all be on it. The sooner David and Laura get used to the idea of Kathleen, the easier it will be for all of us."

He reached into his pocket and extracted a small band of gold, which David immediately recognized as his father's wedding ring. He dropped it onto the table and the silver moonlight bounced off the gold. "I'm thinking about divorce. If those kids mean so much to you, then help them to see it my way."

Aunt Jennifer sighed deeply and pushed her chair in. "All right, John, you leave me no choice. But for the record, this is all wrong. There are other ways, if only you'd hear me out …"

David's father raised his hand and shook his head.

"… but since you won't," she continued, "I'll do as you ask. It's as if you hardly know your children anymore." She picked up the candle and stared bleakly at her brother-in-law. "I'll speak to them in the morning." The flickering flame cast dark shadows over her resigned expression. "I'm so sorry, John — for all of you."

David squeezed back into the shadows, his heart thumping in his chest. *Divorce? His father had given up on his mother!*

"Wait, Jennifer. One more thing." His dad motioned her to sit again. "Have you ever considered that Elizabeth's condition might be genetic? I've heard that, well, that mental illness runs in families. You know, if a parent suffers from depression, the children are at a higher risk … I'm afraid. Is there any history in your family?"

The shadows on Aunt Jennifer's face darkened. "No one in our family," she whispered inaudibly.

"Pardon?" David's father leaned toward her.

"I said, no one in our family. It's ridiculous. We control our own fate."

"I have heard rumours — your father, the children's grandfather. I never knew him. There were rumours that he … well, to put it plainly, didn't die a natural death … suicide. Were those rumours based on truth?" David flinched at the anger in his father's voice. "Before I married into your family, one of you should have told me."

"Would it have made any difference?" Aunt Jennifer said flatly.

"Probably not. I loved her. But we might have made different decisions. About kids. What about David and Laura? What if there is something to all this genetic stuff you hear?"

Aunt Jennifer had visibly paled. "There isn't. I don't believe it. I don't think you have a thing to worry about." She sniffled and stood stiffly. "I'm sorry, John." She turned and bolted from the table, sweeping by David's hiding place, blinded by her tears.

David froze. Out on the bay, Clapper smacked his flipper against the surface of the water and the sound echoed through the night. A low moan escaped his father's lips and David pushed his fingers to his ears. Adults aren't supposed to cry, he told himself, but he knew it was just one more lie.

He waited in the cool darkness until his dad had gone to bed and then he crept stealthily back to his own room. Laura lay sound asleep curled around her doll, her breathing deep and even. David watched her, unwilling to wake her until he had to. He stood there and thought about everything he had overheard between his father and his aunt.

He did know a little bit about genes and DNA. Genes carry hereditary information, information that was passed on from one generation to the next. He knew from science class that he was a combination of his mother's and his father's genes. His dad seemed to think that maybe it was his mother's genes that caused her depression, and that perhaps he and Laura might one day suffer the same fate. Aunt Jennifer hadn't really confirmed or denied how his grandfather had died, but what if it had been suicide?

David shook his head. He'd never, even at his lowest points, considered taking his own life. Somehow his dad had got it all wrong, like he'd got everything else wrong. The one thing David knew for sure was that he wasn't ready to return to Toronto, not yet and maybe not ever. He was happier on Fern Island than he'd been in a long time, and he wasn't ready to give that up yet.

There was little time to waste. It was already one o'clock in the morning. The Daddy plane would be on the island in about forty hours, and David and Laura would not be on it. They could wait until daylight or flee now. If they left now, the moon would light their way, and besides, nobody would notice them missing until eight-thirty or nine o'clock in the morning at the earliest. That gave them, David reckoned, almost eight hours to make their escape. He didn't want to spend another minute under the same roof as his father, his aunt and Kathleen. All of them, in their own way, had betrayed him, or were willing to. There was no one left to trust but himself. His plan was risky, but staying here after all he'd heard would be like walking into a trap.

David lit the coal-oil lamp and dug their backpacks out from under the bunk bed. He rummaged through the closet and found two old sleeping bags. They were bulky and would be awkward to carry, but that was better than being cold. They wouldn't need a tent, not where they were going, and even if they did David didn't know where he'd find one. Both he and Laura had flashlights, and he raided the drawers in the bunkhouse for matches. He chose their clothes carefully, aware that Laura couldn't carry a heavy load.

Besides the clothes they'd wear, David packed each of them an extra pair of cargo pants, two pairs of socks, a wool sweater and a rain jacket. He stuffed the small first-aid kit that sat on the bathroom shelf into his own backpack, as well as the Swiss Army knife his dad had given him on his last birthday. He didn't like to take anything that didn't belong to him, but he decided to "borrow" Aunt Jennifer's fishing rod, two buzz bombs for bait and a handful of hooks.

Getting food proved more difficult. It meant sneaking into the kitchen in the main cabin without waking his aunt, his father or Kathleen. He waited a little longer to be sure they were sound asleep. By five minutes after two, he reasoned the coast was clear. He crept into the main house, terrified he'd wake his father and Kathleen, but they slept on. In the kitchen, he stuffed as many cans of food as he could carry into a bag, careful to leave everything apparently undisturbed in Aunt Jennifer's large pantry.

Fresh water might be a problem, so he took four bottles of water and some water-purifying pills from the top drawer beside the stove, as well as six Tetra Paks of 1% milk. He felt like a thief. After all, Aunt Jennifer had been kind to them the whole time they had stayed with her at Bliss Cove. He picked up a pen to start a note, but did not get past, *Dear Dad*. What could he say that his father, or anyone, could understand?

At twenty past two he was ready. He woke Laura, warning her to be as quiet as possible. "Get dressed in your warmest clothes," he ordered, "and your runners, not your sandals." When she was ready, sleepy-eyed and confused, he thrust a lifejacket into her hands. "Put this on. Don't talk. I promise I'll explain everything as soon as we're out of earshot of the cabin. Trust me. It's an emergency. Don't forget Susie."

He zipped up his own Mustang vest, and they sneaked out into the damp night. Impulsively, he picked up his father's wedding ring as they tiptoed by the table. It was cold to touch and he slipped it into his pocket. Taking Laura by the hand, he guided her past the arbutus tree and down the stairs. The canopy of trees overhead blocked the moonlight, and David didn't want to use their flashlights until they were a safe distance away. Together, they slid down the steep path, feeling their way through the inky darkness toward the sound of the breaking waves.

I won't let them take us away, David promised himself. When Paul's plane leaves Fern Island tomorrow afternoon, Laura and I will be long gone!

Chapter Ten

WHEN they were well away from the cabin, treading across the moonlit beach, David told Laura almost everything he'd overheard. "Dad says he's divorcing Mum. He wants to take us back to Toronto on Sunday, to live with him and Kathleen. I don't know what's going to happen to Mum." His shoulders slumped. He didn't tell her the things they'd said about his mother. One day she'd have a right to know, but not now, not until he understood more.

"Where are we going?" Laura repeated for the third time. "Why are we running away? Why don't we just tell them we want to stay with Aunt Jennifer?"

"Aunt Jennifer has to do what Dad says. She said we're not her children and she has no choice, so she'll help him. We have to run away so we'll miss the Daddy plane. I think Dad will send Kathleen back to Toronto and he'll stay and help look for us. If nothing else, we're buying time."

"But where are we going?" Laura persisted. She stopped walking. "I'm not moving another step until you tell me where we're going."

David dug his flashlight out of his backpack. The moon would not light their way across the heavily treed island path. "Over to Drifter McGee's."

"Forget it," said Laura. "I'm not going there. He's mean and crazy. Matthew said so. I want to go home." She started to cry.

"Drifter has a dinghy tied up to a log on the beach," David explained. "We need it."

"But he lives on the other side of the island. He'll kill us if he catches us stealing his boat. Besides, why do we need a boat?"

David saw that dark circles framed his sister's large eyes. She looked bewildered. He gripped her shoulders and bent down to her eye level. "Drifter is half-deaf, he won't hear us. We're going to *borrow* his boat and take it to Dragon Island. It's close to Fern. I've seen it from the air. Paul told me all about it. No one lives there and there are caves we can hide in. It might be fun," he added lamely.

"Daddy would never divorce Mummy," Laura said defiantly.

"Laura, you can come with me or you can go back to the cabin and get on that plane and find out for yourself what he plans to do." He rocked back on his heels. "Your call."

She had to make up her own mind. He wasn't willing to kidnap her. Somewhere in the trees, an owl hooted, shattering the night quiet. Laura hoisted her pack onto her shoulders. "It really might be fun," she declared. "Let's go." She started over the path ahead of him.

David grinned. That was his little sister for you — the risk-taker! He caught up to her, taking her hand. "Hold on to me. I know the path pretty well. We're almost halfway there."

Horseshoe-shaped Sand Dollar Bay lay directly opposite Bliss Cove, a short distance as the crow flies, but the footpath wound down to the southern tip of Fern Island, skirting the rocks protruding out of the centre of the island before doubling back to the sheltered bay. Named for its abundance of sand dollars, the beach was often littered with the discarded husks of the small round creatures — each one decorated with a delicate, flower-shaped etching. Over the summer, David had collected dozens of them to take back to Toronto.

He and Matthew had cycled and walked this same path many times, but only in daylight, and unencumbered by heavy backpacks. It was altogether different in the dead of the night. Spooky. The trees became dreadful creatures: their branches were twisted and gnarled arms that clawed at their faces, their roots obstacles to trip them up. For Laura's sake, David put on a brave face, reassuring his sister with a bravado he didn't feel. Every time a twig snapped or an owl hooted from the depths of the tangled forest, his stomach lurched.

When at last the trees thinned and opened onto Sand Dollar Bay, Laura dropped to the ground, fed up. "This had better be it," she snapped.

David nodded toward the old aluminum dinghy that sat high on the beach in the low tide. "It is," he answered, "but it'll take the two of us to get the boat to the waterline."

Drifter McGee's cabin lay in absolute darkness. "I think we're safe. He's asleep," said Laura.

David agreed, glad to be out of the forest and under the moonlight. He stood for a moment to get his bearings. The dinghy was tied to a monstrous old cedar that had long ago washed up onto the beach, becoming a part of the landscape. "Stay right behind me and walk softly," David cautioned Laura. "We can't risk waking up Drifter."

Taking the dinghy out at night was risky. Sand Dollar Bay, protected by a rocky reef on both sides, was relatively calm, but the gap leading to the ocean was shallow and narrow. David studied the water. The tide had begun to rise and they would be running against it. A brisk wind opposed the tide and would be piling up waves at the gap.

They stumbled over the beach to the cedar and easily slipped the dinghy from its mooring. "If only we had a few more hours, the boat would be afloat," David moaned, "but we'll have to drag her down the shore."

They loaded their supplies into the small boat, putting them all on the stern bench so they'd stay dry. "The oars are both here," whispered Laura.

"Good," replied David. "We'll row out of earshot before trying the outboard." He checked the fuel tank. The gauge was at the half mark.

Hauling the dinghy to the water's edge proved to be a difficult task. The boat didn't slide easily over the pebbly sand, and the aluminum hull echoed the scraping like a drum, but the breaking surf muffled the sound and at last they reached the shoreline.

"You get in first," David directed, pausing for breath. "Sit in the stern. You'll have to move the packs to one side." Laura did as she was told, hesitating only to take Susie from her pack. "I'll push off." He shoved the boat out, soaking his runners and his jeans to the knees, until finally they were afloat. He leapt in, settling himself on the hard middle bench. The boat immediately bottomed out. David stuck an oar into the sand and pushed hard. The boat moved reluctantly into the creeping tide, free from land.

Both children glanced nervously toward Drifter's shack but it remained utterly dark and still. "Shh," David mouthed, just to be safe. "Sound travels over water."

He rowed skilfully, dipping the oars soundlessly into the water. "How long do we have to row?" Laura asked.

"We?" David rolled his eyes, concentrating on his rowing, careful that the oars did not jump out of the oarlocks and bang against the gunwales. He quickly fell into a rhythm. Keeping his eyes glued on Drifter's cabin, he rowed steadily, past Drifter's fishboat floating just beyond the tide line, on the lookout for any sudden lights on the beach. As they moved farther from the beach, David began to feel safer, although his shoulders soon ached with the effort of propelling the heavy boat through the water.

Laura huddled in the stern, her arms wrapped around her doll, her eyes also on the beach. "What's that noise?" she whispered.

David stopped rowing, eased the oars out of the water, and listened. "Waves," he said worriedly. "Crashing against the rocks. We're near the mouth." Ahead of them, the spilling water shimmered in the moonlight.

"It's getting louder," Laura said. Her eyes opened wide. "We're going in there? Have you ever done this before?"

"Not exactly," David replied. "But Drifter does it all the time." *In his much bigger boat*, he thought to himself. "You're not afraid, are you?" he challenged.

"No," Laura said. "Susie is." She hugged her doll to her body. "When are we going to start the engine?"

"Now," he replied, guessing they were well out of earshot. They were close to the narrow passage between the rocks. "Switch seats." He moved to the stern of the boat and lowered the engine carefully into the water. "Don't worry," he said, voicing his own concern, "I know how to do this and nobody will hear us over that."

"That" was the pounding roar of the incoming tide colliding with the rocks. "It'll be a bit rough through the gap," David warned, alarmed at the jerky motion of the boat. "Make sure you hold on tight. Once through, we'll hug the shoreline before we make the crossing to Dragon. It's not far."

He squeezed the primer bulb, twisted the throttle to "start" and yanked the starter cord. The engine sputtered and coughed but did not start.

"Hurry up," hissed Laura. "Drifter will hear us!"

David cursed and tried again. The engine hiccupped and roared to life. "Thank God." He snapped the gearshift to forward and twisted the throttle, pointing the bow of the boat into the channel. He braced himself for the rough ride ahead. The little boat bucked and shook, valiantly meeting the incoming tide head on.

David was not prepared for the fierceness of the water flowing through the gap. It churned beneath them, tossing the boat every which way. A short steep wave caught them head-on and a surge of cold water broke over the bow. The boat slewed sideways and David pushed the throttle arm away from his body, fighting to stay on course. Laura, soaked, her feet in a pool of water, screamed.

"Get down!" David yelled at her. "Get right down into the bottom of the boat."

They hung dizzily on the crest of the wave before crashing back down into the well. David threw his whole body weight into controlling the motor. He shoved the steering arm hard to the right, straightening the boat to meet an oncoming wave. The motor shuddered in his hand.

When the next wave hit them, David was ready. Gritting his teeth in determination, he plowed the boat into the swell, willing her forward. He tightened his grip on the motor and held his course even as another wave washed over the bow, soaking the already terrified Laura.

"We're almost through the gap, Laura. Hang in there!" David shouted at his sister. "Stay down!" He was horrified she might fall overboard into the rough sea.

A quick glance back from where they'd come from revealed neither land nor light. They were committed now, more than swimming distance from the shoreline. Capsizing meant they wouldn't survive. The deadly reef rose up on either side of them, but its bulk lay below the water's surface. David had to avoid the rocks and steer the boat out to the calmer water that lay just beyond the bow.

He held his course, colliding head-on into each successive wave and riding it out. At last, the sea became less and less choppy, the whitecaps turned into gentle swells and they were safely out of the bay.

Behind them, the ocean pounded the rocky reef as it had done for centuries. They had taken a risk and won. Beneath the dinghy, the waves rolled soothingly. Exhausted, David set the course in the general direction of Dragon Island, then turned his attention to his sister.

She lay curled in the bilge, clutching her doll, the cold water washing around her shivering body. David couldn't tell if she was cold or terrified or both. "Laura?"

"Are we safe?" she asked.

"We have to get warm. Come on, sit back up on your seat." David indicated the backpacks with a nod. "See if you can dig out some dry clothes."

She did as she was told, rummaging through the packs until she found their sweaters and windbreakers. They stripped off their wet tops and sweatshirts and pulled heavy wool sweaters on over their heads. For once, David welcomed the itchy wool against his cold skin. Hypothermia, he knew, could kill as easily as a rogue wave.

Small islands of every size and description dot Desolation Sound. Together, David and Matthew had explored some of those that lay in close proximity to Fern Island, in Aunt Jennifer's aluminum boat. David had never set foot on Dragon, but he'd listened to Matthew's description of the caves carved out of the cliffs on the east side. Now he struggled to remember those conversations and Paul's words on the day they'd flown over the island. The most important piece of information was that any approach to Dragon needed to be executed on the west and most protected side of the island.

For half an hour, they motored north, skimming across the water, hugging the shores of other islands whenever possible. David had no difficulty seeing, thanks to the silver bands of light that emanated from the clear, bright sky. He listened fearfully for the loud throb of Drifter's boat, but heard nothing. They'd made a clean escape.

"I don't know why you're so worried," said Laura logically. "Even if he heard us leave, he has no way of getting out to his fishboat, because we have his boat. Boy, will he be mad. Everyone will be mad at us, especially Dad."

"No, Laura. You've got it backward. We are mad at *him*!"

They powered ahead in silence, on the lookout for deadheads or other boat traffic, but the night was quiet. Occasionally they spotted cabin lights flickering in the distance, and once the bright flames of a bonfire on a beach. David knew that dawn would bring out fishing boats, but he and Laura would be well hidden by that time.

"How much farther?" Laura asked.

"See for yourself. We're almost there. In fact ... land ahoy!" He pointed off the port side. Dragon Island loomed before them, a dark mass crouched in the silvery sea. "Dragon Island."

"Are there ... ?"

"No, Laura, no dragons — just a warm, safe place for us to hide for a while."

He cut the engine two metres from shore and the boat drifted onto a sloping beach blanketed in perfectly round pebbles. Laura, thrilled to be ashore, jumped out of the dinghy into ankle-deep water, holding the bow line firmly in hand. The water exploded into luminous green around her feet.

"David," she gasped, bending to dip her hands into the glittering water. It cascaded through her fingers, each drop a brilliant aqua-green. "Wow, I've never seen anything so amazing!"

David followed her, stepping into the unexpected light show. "It's the same colour as the glow-in-the-dark stickers on your bedroom ceiling in Toronto."

Delighted, Laura flicked the water, sending sparkles of light into the air. "Do you know what it is?"

David groped around his feet until he retrieved a smooth, flat stone, perfect for skipping. He sent it dancing across the water's surface, leaving a shimmering trail in its wake. "It's phosphorescent algae," he said. "I've heard about it, but I never thought I'd see it."

"It's magic."

"It's an omen. A good omen."

Spellbound, they stood wordlessly on the beach, forgetting for the moment everything but the dancing specks of light. Even the softly breaking waves of the incoming tide spilled iridescence at their feet.

It was the cold that brought them back to the present. The icy fingers of the Pacific propelled David into action. He dragged the boat up onto the beach, and urged Laura to help unload their supplies. Tired and cold now, she complained until David agreed they could leave all but one of the water bottles and the fishing gear in the safety of the boat. "We'll come back for them tomorrow. I don't want to have to make two trips tonight either."

They secured Drifter's boat to a tree, then gathered armfuls of ferns and pieces of bark and driftwood, which they heaped over the boat until it became just another pile of beach debris. The strenuous physical work kept the cold at bay, but exhaustion and creeping cold threatened to overwhelm them.

David had forgotten his watch, but the faint light in the eastern sky hinted at a quickly approaching dawn. They loaded their packs onto weary bodies and started off across the tiny island.

"I don't see why we can't sleep here," Laura grumbled. "I'm tired."

"Because I know a better place," said David, "where no one will ever find us unless we want them to. It's not that far. This is a really small island. Come on," he encouraged, "follow me." He swung his flashlight beam up the beach, and aimed it eastward. "We'll cut across once we find a deer trail."

The back of the dragon's head, David's intended destination, faced west toward the mainland's Coast Mountains. Lofty cliffs, shaped by centuries of winter storms, rose from the floor of the ocean to create a formidable wall of rock on Dragon's west side. It was here, tucked away from sight and sheltered from the elements, that David led his sister, guided by instinct and the limited knowledge he'd garnered of the island.

Tramping over the back of the island on barely discernible deer tracks in semi-light proved difficult. It took twice as long as David had imagined it would. A tangle of deadfall littered the forest floor. New trees sprouted out of rotting fallen trunks. The deer paths did not follow straight lines and were often impossible to locate. Then they had to climb over or crawl under the jungle of branches, ferns and decaying wood that blocked their way. Fifty years ago, Dragon Island had been logged and the second-growth forest had sprouted out of the mess the logging company left behind. They were exhausted and hot, scraped and bruised when they finally reached the other side of the island.

It proved even more challenging to locate a suitable cave to sleep in. They had to approach the pockmarked rocks from below, which meant clambering halfway down the steep trail to just above the treeline. David left Laura with their packs, but soon returned jubilant.

"I've found the perfect place," he said. "It's a bit of a trick getting into the cave, but I'll be right behind you, to boost you over the fallen trees and overhanging rock. Once you're up, I'll pass you our stuff."

But David didn't have the strength to lift Laura high enough. "I just can't reach the ledge," she said shakily.

He lowered her to the ground, near collapse himself.

"Maybe if you stood on a rock or a stump or something," Laura suggested.

"You're brilliant." He hugged her. Together they rolled a log under the ledge, then David balanced on the log, Laura balanced on David and she was up on the second try.

Next, David passed up their gear, along with the fishing rod and the bottle of water they hadn't left in the boat.

"Do you see the cave?" David asked.

"I see a big ledge covered in little trees, and blackberries and …" her voice disappeared for a second and then came back excitedly. "A cave. It's perfect! How will you get up?"

"Lean down. I'll grab your hands. You pull and I'll scramble. We'll do it."

"But I'm too tired to pull you up." Laura sounded near tears.

"It's the last thing you have to do," David pleaded, "and then we can sleep. You don't want to sleep in the cave by yourself, do you?" he threatened, hoping to frighten her into action.

But Laura didn't have the strength or the arm length to pull her brother up. Finally, they gave up.

"I'll go back to the boat and get the mooring lines," David said. "You'll have to stay here. It'll be okay." He regretted his threat to leave her alone.

"I don't want to stay in here alone." Laura began to cry.

"Just lie down in your sleeping bag with Susie and wait for me. It's hardly even dark. The sun will be up soon, and you'll be able to see it rise. I'll be a lot quicker on my own."

"All right," she reluctantly agreed, too tired to argue. "But hurry."

The trek to the other side of Dragon Island was much easier alone and without a load to carry. David made good time. At the boat, he grabbed two more water bottles and the mooring lines. Laura was asleep when he returned, and he had no choice but to wake her so she could attach the rope to a tree. He quickly scrambled up to the cave.

The roomy cavern lay hidden behind a tangle of blackberry brambles, which caught on their clothes and tore at their skin when they scrambled inside, but effectively concealed the entrance. David pulled up the rope, then stripped off his wet jeans and climbed into his sleeping bag, completely worn out. Both children were asleep in seconds while beyond the curtain of blackberry bushes the orange sun climbed slowly over the horizon.

Chapter Eleven

DAVID slept heavily until mid-morning, and would have slept longer if it weren't for the hard, uneven cave floor beneath him. When he opened his eyes, he didn't remember where he was, then the events of last night came flooding back to him. He reached over and shook Laura gently. "Wake up."

Laura rubbed her eyes and sat up groggily. "It's true, then," she said. "I thought maybe I'd dreamt everything." She shifted her weight and reached under her sleeping bag. "Look at this." She held up a jagged rock. "No wonder I'm hurting. I must have been really tired to fall asleep on this."

They didn't bother to get out of their sleeping bags, but opened a can of beans for breakfast and ate them cold, straight out of the can. Neither spoke much at first, both lost in their own private thoughts.

"What time do you think it is, David?" Laura licked the last of the beans off her fingers. "This is really disgusting."

"I don't have a clue. I forgot my watch and the cutlery."

David parted the bramble curtain, inviting the sunlight to stream into their cave. Far below, the water slid in and out against the rocky cliff. "The sun is pretty high in the sky. I bet it's close to noon." Cautiously, he let go the thorny branches and wiggled back into the cave.

"Do you think Dad and Aunt Jennifer have noticed us missing yet?"

"Probably," David said shortly, slightly overwhelmed by their successful middle-of-the-night flight. "We'll have to be really careful outside. If we see a boat, any boat, we duck into the woods. I don't want to be discovered until long after the Daddy plane takes off."

"They'll worry so much," said Laura. She climbed out of her sleeping bag and stretched. "I have to go to the bathroom, if I can get through this bush without tearing the skin off my arms."

David helped her. He stuck his hand gingerly into their tangled doorway and separated the brambles. "Let them worry," he said with more conviction than he felt.

A small sliver of guilt had begun to worm its way into his consciousness. After all, he'd run off with Laura in the dead of the night, without having thought everything through clearly. Aunt Jennifer would be frantic with worry once she discovered their escape, and maybe Kathleen wouldn't leave Fern Island with Paul. Matthew would probably guess where they'd gone. After all, they'd been talking about skipping over to Dragon Island for weeks. Would he tell? Maybe running away was just stupid, and useless. Nothing he did was going to cure his mother or reunite his family.

When Laura returned, David went out to relieve himself. Then they unloaded their backpacks, arranging the food and water in the back of the cave, where it was cool and damp. They spread last night's still-wet clothes over the sun-baked rocks outside the cave entrance, then sat down in the heat.

David turned to Laura. "If you had the power to discover the future, would you use it?"

Laura wrinkled her brow. "What do you mean?"

"If Mum knew she was going to get sick, maybe she wouldn't have had us. Do you think you'd want to know?"

"Yeah, I think I would," Laura answered matter-of-factly. "What about you?"

"I don't know," David answered, avoiding her eyes. "I mean, I don't know anything about my future right now. I don't know what I want to be when I grow up, or where I'll live, or if Dad will marry Kathleen, or even if any of it matters …"

"Or if Mum is ever going to be normal again … that's what you're really thinking about, isn't it? That, and if one of us might turn out like her." It was a statement, not a question, and she added sadly, "I don't know either."

Surprised, David met her eyes. "You mean you know about the whole gene thing?"

"I heard Aunt Jennifer and Daddy talking, too, David. You don't really think I'd take off in the middle of the night just because you told me to? I'm not an idiot, or a baby for that matter. I'm eleven now, remember."

"So you knew! Why didn't you stop me last night when I wasted all that time telling you everything I'd overheard?" David said, irritated.

"Not *everything*," Laura crossed her arms and looked at her brother accusingly. "Anyway, I figured we'd talk about it sometime."

David broke into a rueful smile. "You don't seem too concerned about a possible future spent locked up in your bedroom crying."

"I'm here, aren't I?" Laura sighed. "I believe what Aunt Jennifer said. We make our own future. Besides, we're lucky. We know what to watch out for. Luckier than Mum. I don't think she ever saw it coming. Not really. Sometimes I think we could have done more … you know … I mean in the beginning."

David shook his head and punched Laura playfully on her arm. Surprised was the only way he could describe his reaction to her words. Surprised and proud of her. She'd acted more maturely than he had all along. He lay back on the rocks and closed his eyes. Soon the sun would be dipping into the west, but at the moment it sat directly overhead. David guessed it was close to one o'clock.

"I still don't get it," he puzzled. "Why did you come with me? You seem to have figured everything out, and you like Kathleen."

"Well, I couldn't let you come alone," she laughed. "And besides, even if I like Kathleen, I don't want to live with her. I knew Dad wouldn't listen to us unless we did something drastic."

Laura, David realized, had left her doll in the cave. He'd rarely seen her without the doll at her side. She seemed different some- how — not just his pesty little sister, but a person he was actually talking to, and about the most important person in their world: their mother. He felt different, too, less unsure of himself, and more confident that he'd been right to run. Maybe he did have bad genes, like his father thought, but he also had a say in his own future. He'd live life as he pleased, without fear.

"Sometimes when I think of Mum at home without us, I feel so guilty," he confessed. "I wish there was another way."

"Me, too," agreed Laura. She stood and peered over the rocky ledge. "Let's explore." She wrapped the mooring rope around her fist and lowered herself down the rock face with all the agility of a monkey.

David followed, making a silent promise to himself to stop being fearful, to take more risks. For starters, he'd shinny up the old tree in their backyard in Toronto as soon as they got home.

They'd decided over breakfast to gather cedar boughs from a recently fallen tree as well as some soft moss to make their beds more comfortable. Although they'd debated collecting firewood, they'd decided a fire, even a tiny one, would be too risky. "Why did we bring fishing rods if we can't cook?" Laura asked. David shrugged. "I wish I'd brought candles instead."

They spent the afternoon lugging their boughs and moss back to the cave. At last, satisfied that their beds were as soft as they'd ever be, they allowed themselves some time to crawl around the shore, looking in tidal pools and exploring the area surrounding their temporary home. All the while, they kept their ears and eyes alert for boats. None appeared.

Both were reluctant to make the difficult trek back across Dragon Island to where they had stashed Drifter's dinghy. If a search party had been sent to hunt for them, they reasoned, they would likely begin their search on the west side of the island, where the beach was suitable for landing boats. Comfort came in the knowledge that the little boat was well disguised. Nobody would guess it lay under the pile of bark and wood among the driftwood that littered the beach.

They ate their dinner perched on the ledge outside the cave, in the early evening shadows. "I never thought cheese and soggy crackers could taste this good," said David, washing the simple food down with gulps of water.

"It doesn't," retorted Laura. "I'd rather be eating blackberry buns. Don't you think it's kind of weird that no one is out look-ing for us?" she added.

David didn't answer immediately. He supposed they were, but just not in the right place. The Pacific was in a quiet mood; not a wave rippled the surface of the green water, flat and still as a mirror. Behind them, the sun began to set, and suddenly cold, he shivered. "Not really," he replied. "Desolation Sound is huge. We could be anywhere."

"Boat!" Laura stood and peered eastward. "Boat! I'm sure I saw a boat or something moving out there!"

David followed her pointing finger, but saw only a delicate pattern of gentle circles, growing progressively larger as they spread out from the centre point. "I thought I heard an engine a second ago, but I don't see anything on the water." The words were hardly out of his mouth when a large, smooth, black head broke the surface of the sea, beneath a spray of water. Killer whale! Another majestic head appeared, this one bursting straight out of the water so the white of its underside could be easily seen. David rose excitedly. "They're spy-hopping."

The two magnificent marine mammals continued to bob in front of them while three more flashed by, their distinctive dorsal fins cutting through the sea as they expelled water out of their blowholes.

"Why are they sticking their heads out of the water?" Laura asked.

"That's how they check their surroundings, what's happening on the surface. I've seen pictures of it, but I never thought I'd see it in the wild!"

The two spy-hopping whales sank back under the sea with a grace that astounded Laura and David. They reappeared minutes later, propelling their massive bodies through the water before diving again. In all, they counted fourteen whales in the pod streaming past Dragon Island. It was too early in the summer for the mammals to be heading south and too late for a northern journey, so David supposed they must be a resident pod.

"Remember what Paul said the first day we arrived on Fern Island? It's good luck to spot killer whales."

"Not for us. Not this time," answered Laura. "Look! We'd better duck out of sight fast."

David realized he had heard the distant sound of motors. Now they powered into sight. Three Zodiacs rounded the south end of Dragon Island, skirting the eastern shore; each one was filled to capacity with passengers dressed in bright survival suits, sporting cameras and binoculars. "Whale watchers!" he shouted. "Quick! Grab your clothes and get into the cave before they see us." Oblivious to the prickly bushes, they scrambled into the safety of their cave.

Parting the brambles cautiously, they peered out, horrified to see the boats heading directly for the pod. "Paul told me they're not supposed to approach from the rear," said David, "and they're getting awfully close. The noise from the engines drives them crazy!"

"Isn't that Drifter McGee's boat?" said Laura as a much bigger boat came into view, travelling at full throttle.

"He's really moving," said David, as the old fishboat sped across the water on a collision course with the Zodiacs. "What's he up to?"

Drifter passed the inflatable boats, then turned hard in front of them, creating an enormous side wake that would have toppled less stable crafts. He cut his engine suddenly, forcing the Zodiacs to veer sharply off course to avoid a crash. They swung abruptly away from the whales, their captains in shock and passengers screaming.

Drifter paid no attention to their raised fists and angry shouts, but circled the boats slowly. He was yelling something, but David and Laura couldn't hear what it was.

"I think he's protecting the pod." David suddenly felt a great affinity for Drifter. Sure enough, Drifter manoeuvred his boat skilfully so that none of the smaller craft could get any closer to the departing whales. "He'll ram them if they don't back off," said David. The skippers of the Zodiacs must have sensed the same thing. Two of them turned back immediately. The remaining one tried to skirt around the fishing boat in pursuit of the whales, but Drifter turned his boat aggressively toward the black Zodiac, gunned his engine and raced straight at it, swerving hard right at the last moment before they hit. The ensuing wave from the wake nearly swamped the smaller craft. Amid angry shouts, the water-logged Zodiac turned back in the direction it had come from.

"Way to go, Drifter!" David cheered, while Laura clapped at the receding Zodiacs. "He's not such a crazy guy after all."

"Yeah, but how did he get out to his boat?"

"However he did it," David replied, "he knows the dinghy's gone, but I wonder if he told anyone? He's such a hermit."

"Eventually they'll find out and put two and two together. They've probably spent today combing Fern Island. Aunt Jennifer must be frantic and she's never been anything but nice to us."

"Forget it, Laura," said David. "It's too late for guilt."

"Do you think any of them might guess we've gone to Dragon Island?" David knew by Laura's tone she didn't really want to spend another night in the cave.

"Matthew might, but probably it'll take him a while," replied David. "We're here for tonight. If we hadn't been here, we wouldn't have seen the whales or figured out that Drifter McGee isn't such a bad guy."

Dinner, like breakfast, consisted of a can of cold beans, which they ate with sticks instead of their fingers. As soon as the sun disappeared, a damp chill settled into the cave. David and Laura were quick to climb into their much more comfortable sleeping bags. Laura fell asleep almost immediately, but David couldn't relax. Tomorrow was Sunday. They'd have to be careful to stay hidden until the Daddy plane had taken off, hopefully with Kathleen on board. Monday morning they'd let themselves be found.

David should have felt better than he did. Everything was going according to plan, yet he was plagued with doubts. How would his father react to their running away? What about Aunt Jennifer? Would they be relieved or furious when they found them? Would Kathleen fly home, or stay on Fern Island? Would his father listen to David or just blow him off? He tossed and turned for hours before falling into a troubled sleep.

Chapter Twelve

AUNT Jennifer had slept later than usual, and woke to the cries of the eagles that lived in the great old cedar outside her window. She stayed in bed for a few minutes and listened to them, while yesterday's events — especially the upsetting confrontation with her brother-in-law — paraded through her thoughts. Today, she decided, she would talk to the children, but not before she'd made one more attempt to reason with their father.

Overnight, she'd devised a plan, a possible solution to their dilemma, if only he'd hear her out. Feeling slightly more optimistic, she climbed out of bed and crept softly through the living room, taking care not to wake Kathleen. John wasn't in the cabin. Perhaps, Aunt Jennifer mused, stoking the woodstove to perk coffee, John and the kids had set out on an early-morning walk together. God only knew they needed time alone, time to talk.

All of them had been through so much, especially in the past year when Elizabeth had really lost control of her world. Poor Elizabeth … and Jennifer had done nothing to make it easier for her, had not even recognized how badly she needed help. Her sister's last letters hadn't directly mentioned her fragile mental state, but Aunt Jennifer wished that she'd paid more attention to what wasn't said — to the emptiness and sadness between the hastily penned lines.

And John … he had a right to be afraid for his children, even if it was unnecessary. Jennifer sighed. Today she would tell him the truth, and break the promise she had made long ago to her own, now dead mother.

◑

David and Laura's father had not slept well. He regretted his anger at Jennifer. After all, she'd helped him immensely with the children and had never accused him of abandoning her sister. Not that he'd had any choice, but he felt terrible guilt at the way things had turned out. He had never bargained on meeting Kathleen, and had never meant to fall in love again, if he was really in love at all. It wasn't his fault that the woman he'd married had lost the ability to cope with everyday life.

He awoke before the sun had risen, restless and worried. Didn't his children belong with what was left of their family? Unable to sleep, he rose quietly to avoid waking anyone, dressed, grabbed an apple and crept out of the cabin to be alone with his thoughts.

Standing on the porch, he thought about his sleeping children. He considered waking them to make up for the day before. Maybe they'd go fishing or take a long walk on the beach. He almost went to them, but stopped. It wasn't clear in his mind what he would tell them.

He felt himself poised on the brink of a chasm that stretched between them. He ached to vault over the void, but did not know how. Sighing heavily, he tiptoed off the porch and started down the winding path alone, leaving the heavy imprint of sadness on the soft earth.

He spotted Matthew and his father at the end of the wharf fishing and a fresh wave of guilt washed over him. He didn't really have any right to take David and Laura away from Fern Island, not until summer was over. He owed them some of his own time. It wasn't too late to fix things. The only person on tomorrow's flight to Vancouver, he decided, would be Kathleen. He would stay for as long as he could. He headed off down the beach, lost in his thoughts.

◗

Kathleen, the only person in the cabin who'd slept well, woke to an empty house, but found Jennifer out on the porch. "Good morning," she said. "Where is everybody? It's awfully quiet around here."

"I know," Aunt Jennifer laughed. "It's kind of a treat, isn't it? I'm assuming they've all gone for a walk. Coffee?"

"Please. I had no idea how much noise two children can make!"

Aunt Jennifer excused herself and returned a minute later with a steaming cup of coffee. She hadn't had much time alone with John's girlfriend and felt slightly awkward. "Children certainly take up a lot of space," she said, picking up the thread of conversation. "Either one enjoys them, or one doesn't."

Kathleen laughed. "The jury's out on that, as far as I'm concerned," she said, "but to be honest, two children are definitely two more than I'd ever bargained for."

Jennifer shrugged. *There's my answer,* she thought. "They're great kids, but they've had a hard time. It's a pity John can't stay on a little longer. Even a couple more days would be helpful. They've got a lot of questions and very few answers."

"It was tough for me to get away from the office at all," replied Kathleen, "but as for John, here he comes now. Why don't you put it to him?"

"Put what to me?" David and Laura's dad, flushed from his walk,

pulled out a chair and sat down. "Wait," he smiled. "I have something to put to both of you first." He turned to Jennifer. "But not
until I've apologized for my temper last night. I was out of line."

"Ditto for me," Aunt Jennifer replied. "You see, I too have some
explaining to do. You asked me …"

"Whoa," said John, "Me first! I've done a lot of thinking this
morning. The long and short of it is that my kids need me. I'm
going to let the office know that I need an extra week." He looked
sheepishly at Kathleen. "I'm afraid you'll be travelling home without me tomorrow evening."

Kathleen looked disappointed, but graciously nodded and said
nothing. Aunt Jennifer leaned over and gave her brother-in-law
a grateful hug. "I'm thrilled, John. It's exactly what they need. I
thought a long walk might clear your mind, all of your minds.
Are David and Laura still down at the beach?"

"As far as I know, they're still in bed — and now I think I'll
help myself to a cup of coffee. I'm not used to exercising so early
in the morning."

"On the stove," said Aunt Jennifer absently. "Still in bed? You
mean they weren't with you? They're normally early risers."

"With me?" John shook his head. "I was up and out of here
at the crack of dawn. They're tired after last night. Don't worry.
Let them sleep if they need it."

Aunt Jennifer stood up. "Of course, but I think I'll go and check
on them." She smiled self-consciously. "I'm turning into a real
mother hen!"

"Go ahead," said John. "It's the only way you're going to relax."

"You're right." She walked firmly toward the bunkhouse, determined not to let them see any more of her anxiety, but once
through the door she rushed into David's bedroom.

Empty! Laura's the same. She yanked open the closet door, and saw that the packs and sleeping bags were gone. She felt sick. "John!" she called urgently. "John!" Her legs wobbled beneath her and she sank down on the bed, unable to support her weight. "They're gone," she said, ashen-faced, when their father entered the room. "They've run away. David and Laura have run away."

The three of them combed Fern Island, reassured by the presence of Aunt Jennifer's boat beached in Bliss Cove. By afternoon, Matthew's family had joined in, but there was no sign of David and Laura. Eventually, it was Kathleen who voiced everyone's greatest fear: "They've either left the island or ... Do they ever swim by themselves?"

"They're strong swimmers," snapped Aunt Jennifer, "and they always let someone know where they're going and what they're doing. I refuse to even speculate ..."

"Calm down, Jenn," said John. "We believe you. Obviously they've left Fern Island. But how? Are you sure every boat on the island is accounted for?"

"I've spoken to everyone," said Mr. Bloom. "There are no boats missing. Drifter motored by earlier, and he always tows his dinghy." He placed a reassuring hand on Aunt Jennifer's shoulder. "I'm sure they're okay, but I think it's time to call in the Coast Guard, just to be on the safe side."

"I think we should talk to this Drifter character first," said John, "although by the sounds of him, I think we'd have heard about it if someone stole his boat."

"To set everyone's mind at ease, I'll go over to Drifter's cabin," offered Mr. Bloom.

"He's not as bad as he's made out to be," said Aunt Jennifer, "and besides, if he knew anything, he'd tell us. It's almost dark.

I'm going to radio Paul and ask him to get up here early in the morning. He'll notify the Coast Guard and they'll start a search." Her voice broke and she disappeared into the cabin.

The small group was huddled in despair on the porch, unsure what to do next, when a gruff voice hailed them from the beach trail. "Those kids of yours could be on any island within an hour or two of here. I had to swim out to my trawler and swim back into shore. Just heard about the runaways from the Smiths." It was Drifter McGee, a black look on his grizzled face. "Little delinquents stole my dinghy. I thought I heard noises in the night, should of listened to my gut."

Aunt Jennifer burst out of the cabin, tears streaming down her face.

"Why didn't you tell us earlier?" she cried.

"I had some business out on the water. Couldn't wait. I'm telling you now. Anyway, I hoped I'd catch them myself and give them a piece of my own mind. Kids today are mollycoddled." Drifter glared at them all, turned abruptly and disappeared down the path into the dark.

Chapter Thirteen

"**D**AVID. Wake up! Wake up!" Laura shook her brother.

He opened his eyes, startled. "What? What is it?"

"You were screaming. Really screaming."

David took a deep breath to slow down his racing heart. "I had a bad dream. Really bad, but I can't remember … Is it morning already?"

"A nightmare." Laura nodded knowingly. "How am I supposed to know what time it is? All I know is it's freezing in here."

She was right. Their hiding spot depended on the sun for warmth, but the blackberry bushes grew too thickly to allow any light in. David burrowed down into his sleeping bag. "Go back to sleep. It's too early to wake up.

"I'm not tired. I'm hungry. I'm cold and I don't see the point of staying here any longer. Besides, it's not early, it's just cold in here. Look — the sun is shining on the ledge."

David yawned and sat up. He peeked through the brambles. The morning was almost past. "Okay," he said. "I'm awake. Everything's going to be okay." But he didn't feel okay. He felt tired and his nightmare had spooked him, but for Laura's sake he assumed a confident tone. "I had the same thought. We'll go back to Fern Island tonight. After the plane takes off. At least we've let them know we're not too happy about what's going on."

Breakfast consisted of cold creamed corn, milk and the last of the crackers. Laura wolfed down the meal after declaring, "I'll never eat anything out of a can again! It's totally disgusting," but David didn't feel hungry. He felt guilty. Laura didn't really want to be here, had never wanted to come in the first place, and David's reasons for leaving seemed less and less clear. He rolled up his sleeping bag, slowed by the weight of his responsibility toward his sister. It wasn't a new feeling, nor a welcome one.

"Should we leave our stuff here or come back for it later?" Laura's belongings were piled neatly at the mouth of the cave.

"How should I know?" snapped David. He parted the brambles. "We've got lots of time. Let's go check on the boat … We might as well dump our stuff in it. It's lots warmer outside than it is in here."

He pushed his way through the blackberries, then held them apart for Laura. They lowered themselves over the ledge easily and followed the twisting deer paths back through the damp forest to the western edge of Dragon Island. Twice they spotted deer, curious and unafraid at the unfamiliar sight of two-legged intruders.

When they arrived at the protected beach, the tide was still creeping out. Drifter's boat, which they'd left just above the waterline, lay quite high up and dry on the rocky beach.

"It's okay." David began to uncover the buried boat and Laura joined him. "By afternoon the tide will have risen and it will be a piece of cake to launch the boat. Don't the tides seem really extreme to you?"

"Cusp of a full moon."

David turned puzzled eyes on his sister.

"Aunt Jennifer told me that on full-moon nights the tides are extra high and extra low."

"Okay. It's a good thing we weren't going anywhere in a hurry 'cause we'd never get the boat down to the water."

"Let's try anyway."

They loaded their packs and the little bit of food left into the boat. A stately blue heron eyed them from a safe vantage point while they pushed, pulled and dragged the dinghy over the pebbles, gaining only a short distance before giving up.

"This is hopeless and stupid," said David. "We'll just wait until the tide comes in."

To the west a wall of black clouds had begun to gather. "I hope it'll stay dry until then. It looks like rain," said Laura.

"Remember what Paul said. There's a halo of sunshine over Fern Island." David looked doubtfully at the incoming weather. "But I guess there's always an exception to the rule."

They beachcombed for a while, crawling among the driftwood collecting skipping rocks and interesting pieces of wood to take home, then David suggested they explore Dragon Island, taking advantage of the low tide to follow the beach.

"We'll pretend we're shipwrecked, that we don't have any way of getting off the island and we're all by ourselves," Laura beamed.

"In case you haven't noticed," David pointed out, "that's pretty close to the truth!"

She stuck her tongue out at him. "Okay, know-it-all. Let's go."

"All right, but let's backtrack across the island and then work our way back over here. Otherwise it'll get late, and I don't want to hurry."

They'd already walked a fair way down the beach, so they entered the woods in an open spot, assuming they would easily pick up another deer trail. They didn't find one and crossing Dragon proved to be more difficult than they would have anticipated on such a small island. It took twice as long as it had earlier. A tangle of deadfall littered the forest floor, making it impossible for them to walk in a straight line. They had to climb over or crawl under the jungle of branches, ferns and new growth blocking their way. They arrived on the east side of the island hot, bruised and scratched.

"Water!" Laura groaned, flopping onto the stones. "The rocks are warm," she added, picking up a handful and spreading them over her legs.

David joined her. "Look. I … uh … we forgot the water. It's still in the bottom of the boat. I'm thirsty, too!"

Laura glared at him. "I'm dying of heat." She took off her shoes, flung them aside and walked down to the waves. "Wanna go swimming?" She stuck her toes into the breaking water.

They paddled in the shallows until they'd cooled off. The sun disappeared behind a cloud, but the rocks retained the solar heat. They stretched out on them until warmth returned to their bodies. In the distance they heard the steady hum of boat engines and David speculated a search party had been launched.

"This time, if we see a boat, we get their attention," he declared.

Thirsty and now hungry, too, they decided to return to the boat and their dwindling supplies. They set off across the rocky beach. It was difficult walking and their feet sank heavily into the stones, but they pushed forward in the afternoon heat.

Earlier, Laura had suggested they map out the island while they walked, giving names to the various points and coves along the way. Although David had agreed enthusiastically, both were too tired to bother.

Several times they had no choice but to clamber over boulders and trees that blocked their path. Eventually they arrived at a rocky bluff rising sharply out of the forest and extending far out into the sea. David sat down, discouraged, beneath the intimidating wall of rock. They'd have to climb over it or go back the way they'd come.

"Now what?" said Laura. "I'm not going back and I'm not climbing a cliff. I'm tired and I want a drink."

"Take a break," advised David. "It looks worse than it is. I'm sure we can get over it. We're more than halfway back to the boat. I'm not turning back. It'll take way too long."

He looked out to sea, to the incoming tide. Some of their footprints had already been erased by the waves. He hoped the boat would be okay where they'd left it.

"We'll rest for a few minutes," he decided. "And when we're rested, we'll continue up and over the rock."

He squatted down beside Laura and began to clear the pebbles away in a small square. "Let's draw a map of the island."

They used sharp sticks to trace lines in the wet sand, outlining the contours of Dragon Island. Naming the coves, trails, caves and forests they'd discovered became a game and took their minds off the climb ahead, their burning thirst and empty stomachs.

"The trail across the island is Skull and Dagger Way," said Laura.

"That's babyish," retorted David.

"How about Woodland Wonder?"

David rolled his eyes and so it went. They argued about the name of every landmark until they grew irresistibly sleepy in the afternoon sun. Bit by bit, the tide crept up the beach, reclaiming the chunks of driftwood it had deposited there hours earlier. David and Laura dozed on the still-warm pebbles. The first to wake up, David discovered their map semi-submerged in water and the sun completely obliterated by dark clouds. He had no way of estimating the time.

"Laura!" He shook her urgently. "Come on, Laura! Wake up! We have to get back to the boat before it's cast adrift!"

Laura startled awake. "I'm freezing."

"You'll warm up scaling the cliff. Do you think you can do it?"

"You're the one who's always been afraid of climbing," Laura scoffed.

David nodded, remembering the old tree in their backyard in Toronto. "Not any more," he said and started up the bluff, thinking of the water bottle in the bottom of the boat and not looking down.

Laura followed close behind him. The first section was easy, as the rocks rose gently and small shrubs provided strong handholds. David climbed slowly, picking his route carefully and stopping periodically under the pretence of ensuring that Laura was okay. In fact, the pauses were to steady his own nerves. His dislike of heights hadn't lessened in spite of his determination to live fearlessly.

He'd hoped to stay closer inland, but the slope forced him to pick a route nearer the incoming surf.

"Be careful," he called down to Laura. "It's slippery where the rocks are wet. Stay away from the green, slimy ones if you can."

"That's kind of hard! They're all green and slimy. You're picking the path!"

David stopped. His arms ached. The cliff was higher than he'd thought. Above him, the rocks in this section soared vertically. He scrambled for a footing, slipped and smashed his knee against the hard surface. "Ouch!"

A shower of small stones rained down on Laura. "Watch it!" she yelled up at him.

"Sorry," he called down, shaken. "I'll take it slower over the next part … unless you think we should go back down?"

"I'm fine. Aren't you?"

David kept moving up and out toward where the waves broke over the rocks below them. Salty spray licked his skin, making him itchy and more determined to get out of the reach of the surf. Finally he hoisted himself up onto a tiny horizontal ledge and stopped to rest, peering down at his sister. He'd made it more than halfway up, three-quarters. He'd climbed! He'd done it!

But something in Laura's body language checked his triumph. She appeared frozen on the rock, her face a pale shade of grey. "Climb, Laura," he coaxed.

"I can't. My nose is itchy. I'm scared. I want to scratch it, but I can't let go!"

"As soon as you get to where I am, you can rest and scratch all you want, but don't let go yet. There's a handhold, a branch, right above your right hand. Grab onto it and I'll reach down and pull you up."

"But I'm scared."

"Come on, Laura, you can do it." David's last words were drowned in the wind and waves and rain. A large rolling breaker slammed into the bluff, only metres below them, sending a flurry of white water into the air and drenching Laura. She cried out.

"Laura, it's gusting. The tide's coming up fast. Climb! Now!" David urged, leaning as far over the tiny ledge as he could manage.

Laura moved her right hand slowly above her head, groping for the invisible handhold, her fingers scraping over the rough surface. "I can't feel anything!" she wailed. "I'm stuck."

"Just a little higher," David coaxed, but he could see that her arm would fall short of the target. "There's a little tree or shrub beneath the branch. Reach for it!"

Tentatively, she stretched her hand higher, fumbling blindly until her fingers closed over the greenery. "Got it!"

David cupped his hands around his mouth to project his voice over the wind. "Now lift your left foot up." A second wave crashed into the rock, soaking Laura. "Lift your left leg up about six centimetres. There's a little step in the rock. Hurry. It'll get you out of the spray."

"Are you sure?" David had never heard Laura panicked, and it scared him.

"Trust me."

She eased her left leg slowly, propelling herself upward by pulling on the little bush with her right hand. "Don't put all your weight on that shrub!"

David's warning, drowned in the wind, came too late. The shallow roots let go their tenuous hold on the rock, and for a brief second Laura locked her terrified eyes onto David. Then she screamed, lost her balance and fell down the ragged face to the rocks below.

David heard a snap and his stomach turned over. "Laura!" he bellowed. "Laura!"

He scrambled and slid down the incline, oblivious to the jagged rocks and shrubs tearing his skin as he bumped his way to where his sister lay in a crumpled heap on the soggy ground. "Laura! Laura! You're okay. You're okay, aren't you?" The words tumbled out of his mouth incoherently. He knew she wasn't.

She lay still, her eyes wide and tear-filled, her face pinched and chalky white — the colour of fear. "My leg," she moaned. "I've hurt my leg!"

David swallowed the bile pooling in the back of his throat. He'd heard the snap; he already knew. Her left leg lay twisted and limp at an odd angle to her body, like a rag doll's. He thought he might be sick. He looked away, took a deep breath and refocused his attention. No blood. No blood was good. He removed his sweatshirt, rolled it up and placed it beneath Laura's damp head. A long, ugly red scratch fanned over her left eye.

"Your leg is broken," he said softly. "But you'll be okay. I know a little first aid. Don't cry, Laura ..."

"I'm not crying," she groaned. "You are."

David swiped at his wet eyes. "You're right. How bad does it hurt?"

"Pretty bad," she replied. Her eyes closed.

David wrapped his arms around her trembling body. He knew what had to be done. "Laura. Wait." He tore up the beach searching frantically for the right piece of wood. Spotting a long silver slab of cedar, he grabbed it and ran back to her. He ripped off his shirt and tore it into long strips, using them to secure the wood to her leg. "Now, put your arms around my neck. I have to move you away from the water!" He knew that the first rule of first aid was to *not* move a hurt person, but if he didn't the ocean would swallow her.

He opted for speed rather than tenderness, and closing his ears and heart to her cries of pain, half dragged, half carried her as gently as he could to a more sheltered spot beside an ancient, weather-worn log. Laura fainted, and David sat cradling her head until her eyes flickered open.

"Do you trust me?" he said. It seemed an odd question. After all, her trust in him so far had only landed her in deep trouble.

"Like I have a choice," she whispered.

"Laura, I have to get back to the boat. We need food, water and sleeping bags. We need matches for a fire."

"Don't leave me!" she cried. "What if something happens to you? What if you don't come back?" Her face crumpled.

"I'll be back. I swear."

"Pinky swear?"

He locked his baby finger with hers. "Pinky swear." They shook.

Laura smiled wanly. "My leg really hurts."

David made her as comfortable as possible. He calculated he'd be gone for an hour or more if he went the way they'd come, over the bluff. He removed his shoes and tied them together around his neck, reasoning that he'd have a better grip on the cliff, but would need them to sprint across the pebbles. She lay still and quiet and her courage strengthened David's resolve not to panic and make a mistake. David reassured her that she wasn't to worry. He'd take care of things.

He ascended the rock without incident this time, slithered down the other side, slipped into his shoes and hit the beach running.

As he ran, he recreated the map they'd worked on earlier, to distract himself. He'd left Laura in Dog Bay. He'd scaled Shark's Tooth, then sped past a point of land. The dinghy lay in Orca Bay, the next bay. Not far. Or so he hoped. The map had been created from their imaginations, not from fact.

He flew over the beach, over logs and boulders and rocky outcrops, oblivious to anything except the urgency to return to his sister. He ran through the dry pain in his throat and the sand in his eyes. He ran out of the rain and into drizzle that mingled with his own tears. This wasn't a new feeling for David. For a long time now, he and Laura had looked after themselves, without any support. This wasn't new; it was just worse.

The sun, barely visible behind the bank of clouds, had moved across the sky and begun its descent behind Vancouver Island. He had plenty of daylight left, but it was the moon that had betrayed them. The moon, whose invisible pull commanded the tides.

He couldn't see the boat! Heartsick, David scanned the beach before grudgingly turning his eyes to the water. He'd been a fool to leave her untied. There was the dinghy, drifting in the middle of the bay!

David was a good swimmer. Good enough, anyway. He stripped off his jeans and set them down on the beach. The water was frigid, but David was hot and the sea inviting. For ten long minutes he swam against the tide, never losing sight of the supply-filled boat, never forgetting his sister and his promise to return to her.

When his fingers finally closed on the bow, he couldn't find the strength to hoist himself into the boat. The mooring lines, he remembered, were tied to a tree at the foot of the cave. David paddled to the stern and began pushing it slowly ashore, helped now by the incoming tide.

Halfway there, the sound of an engine reached his ears, and minutes later her wake washed over him, but from his vantage point low in the water he saw nothing. David prayed that he'd been spotted, but he had no way of telling.

He beached the boat and secured it to a tree trunk. He paused to gulp down some sweet-tasting water, stuffed matches, the first aid kit and some of Laura's clothes into his backpack, grabbed both sleeping bags and began the long trip back to Dog Bay. His shadow stretched before him, long and thin in the late-day sun. At least the rain had stopped.

Hadn't anyone reported them missing? Didn't they care? Where was the search plane, or the Coast Guard? Come to think of it, David hadn't seen or heard the Daddy plane at all — odd for a Sunday. He hadn't felt this alone since he'd befriended the wolf spider who lived under the back steps of the house in Toronto. Memories of home, sad, lonely memories, flooded back to David. He pushed them aside.

Chapter Fourteen

"**THERE** it is, Dragon Island." Paul banked the little plane hard left. Beside him, buckled into the right seat, Aunt Jennifer clenched and unclenched her fists distractedly. A sheen of nervous perspiration dampened her face as she stared out the window of the Beaver at the small island below.

Paul glanced at her worriedly out of the corner of his eye. He'd never seen her disturbed or even vaguely troubled before and he wished there was something concrete he could do to allay her fears.

He reached out and placed his hand over hers. "Don't worry," he said. "We're going to find them. They're smart kids and they can take care of themselves for a few days."

She dragged her eyes away from the window and looked up at him doubtfully. "I hope you're right, Paul." She squeezed his hand. "I hope you're right."

Paul looked back at the kids' father, John, perched on the edge of his seat, his lips drawn together in a flat, narrow line. Poor guy. He looked like he might fall apart any minute now. "Any sign of them?"

Nobody replied. "Keep looking for Drifter's small boat," he advised.

Seated beside John, Matthew was torn between fear and excitement at being part of the search. Binoculars glued to his eyes, he pored over Dragon Island. "Nothing yet," he reported at regular intervals.

Paul descended another twenty-five metres. "Look again," he said. "I've only got about fifteen minutes left until I'll need to head back to refuel."

"Check the caves on the eastern side," suggested Matthew. "It's too rough to land over there, but if they're on Dragon, that's probably were they would set up camp."

Paul complied and changed course, steering the plane over the island to the eastern shore. The caves were easy to pick out, staring vacantly up at them like empty eye sockets, but they didn't detect any movement or flashes of colour.

"Damn it! Why did they run in the first place? Why didn't they come to me?" The children's father buried his face in his hands. "I just want a second chance."

Aunt Jennifer removed her headphones and turned around to face her brother-in-law. "You'll get your second chance, John. I know you will. Paul's right. They're smart kids. Besides, both of us are to blame. I should have talked to them, seen the signs …"

Matthew shifted uncomfortably, careful to look anywhere but at Mr. Garrett's damp eyes. "Ah, folks," Paul interrupted. "Talk less and look more. I'll do another flyover, but let's face it, if they don't want to be seen, they won't be seen. Anyway, we're not a hundred percent sure they're even on Dragon."

The radio crackled to life. "Uh, Delta Alpha Zulu. This is the Coast Guard. Do you read?"

"Coast Guard, this is Delta Alpha Zulu. Go ahead." Paul identified his plane.

"Delta Alpha Zulu. Are you carrying a GPS? If so, what is your exact position?" The passengers strained to decipher the fuzzy transmission.

Paul read the screen on his handheld global positioning system.

"My position is five zero point two three, north, one two four point one west. Nothing below us but the deep blue sea and a smattering of islands. Directly over Dragon Island and about to do one more flyby, before returning to refuel. Will maintain radio contact. Out."

"Roger, Delta Alpha Zulu." The radio went silent.

Thirty metres below, and slightly south, David and Laura sat in horrified silence as the low hum of the Beaver's engine grew fainter and finally ceased altogether. David had just arrived back at Laura's side. He found her still and quiet, numbed, he supposed, by pain and shock. He'd started to wrap her in her sleeping bag when she lifted her head and whispered, "Do you hear a noise?"

David did. He heard his raspy breath and his heart pounding in his chest. He'd jogged the entire way back. "No," he said and bent to hear her more clearly.

"Listen," she said urgently, her breath hot and feverish against his ear.

"The Beaver!" Too soon! David searched the beach frantically for twigs, dried grasses and small pieces of driftwood. Fire would alert the plane to their location. Fire meant rescue.

Hands shaking, he built the twigs, sticks and grasses into a teepee-shaped cone, then extracted the matches from the bottom of his backpack. They were a bit damp, and he struck ten against the sulphur strip before one lit. He held its weak flame to a handful of grass, coaxing a tiny fire out of the natural wicks, which he then held to the smallest of twigs, blowing gently until they too caught fire.

"They've gone." Laura turned her disappointed face toward the flame. "It's too late."

"They'll be back." *Please God, make them come back.*

But they didn't return, and slowly the daylight began to give way to darkness. David did his best to make Laura comfortable. The first aid kit had not been designed for severe fractures, but he cleaned the cut on Laura's head and bandaged it up. She drank a little water, and David heated the canned pork and beans in the fire for himself. She dozed on and off for the next few hours, but David didn't dare close his eyes for a second, because if he did, he might fall asleep and the fire would go out. They needed it for warmth, but more importantly, they needed it to act as a beacon for their rescuers.

David had a lot of time to think that night on Dragon Island. Some of the things he thought about, he didn't like. He'd run away from his father the same way his father had left them — suddenly and without warning. He worried about his mother, but in truth, he didn't really miss her. He loved her, but he didn't miss her. Did that make him a bad person? He didn't know. While he puzzled over these questions, he fed wormwood into the fire and watched over his sister.

"Come back," he begged aloud at regular intervals. He believed that Paul, if it had been Paul, would return. Sometime in the night he thought he'd imagined the purring sound of the Beaver's engines, but he was too tired and too dejected to believe his own ears.

Laura brought him to his senses. "Can't you hear the airplane?"

"You're awake."

"David. The airplane!"

He shot to his feet as the lights of the Beaver, flying low, appeared from the north. "Down here!" He waved his arms madly. "Down here!"

The plane soared above them, waggled its wings, circled twice and disappeared into the dark.

"We're saved!" David shouted. He danced madly around the fire. Even Laura managed a weak smile through her pain.

Above them, on a return course to Fern Island, Paul barked into his mike. "Coast Guard. Delta Alpha Zulu. Do you read?"

"Delta Alpha Zulu. Go ahead," the Coast Guard's voice crackled over the radio.

"Coast Guard, my position is," Paul glanced at his GPS, "five zero point two one north, one two five point one west. Dragon Island. I've got a fire on the beach and a positive ID of the boy. I know it's dark, but I'm sure it's him. Out."

"Roger. Dragon Island. Is the boy okay? Out."

"He appears to be fine," Paul answered tersely.

"Roger. Thanks, Delta Alpha Zulu. We're on our way. Over."

Paul had been up combing the nearby islands alone for hours. The exhaustion he'd begun to feel was replaced by elation. The kids would be okay. The surge of affection surprised him, though he had long figured out that anything Jennifer liked, he did too. Now he headed back to Fern Island to where Jennifer and John waited expectantly for him on the wharf. He taxied in, but didn't shut down the engines, just gestured for them to climb in. "David's been spotted," he said, as soon as they were belted up safely.

"And Laura?"

"Jennifer, I'm sure she's with him."

"Where?

"On Dragon. I saw flames. They've built a good fire. The Coast Guard's on its way, but I figure we can probably get there faster. There's a cove safe for landing. I'll fly over their location, then I'll let you off, John. You can walk them out to me or wait with them if they need the Coast Guard."

Paul doubled back to Dragon Island, flying at low altitude.

"There's the fire. You see the route to walk around?"

John Garrett nodded. "Thank God for the moon."

Paul landed the Beaver in the cove and beached it. "There's Drifter's dinghy." Aunt Jennifer smiled for the first time. "Those kids are going to be in some kind of trouble with him!"

They hopped out quickly. "Jennifer and I will wait with the plane so that we can direct the Coast Guard. Follow the shoreline?"

"Tell David and Laura I'm cooking a huge breakfast later," Aunt Jennifer said, "so they'd better bring their appetites. And," she added shakily, "tell them both I love them and everything is going to be okay. You tell them that, John. Promise?"

"You have my word. I'll tell them that from both of us."

"You're getting your second chance. Use it well."

"Thanks, Jenn." He kissed her on the cheek, shook Paul's hand and started jogging up the beach, shining his powerful flashlight ahead of him.

●

David heard his father's voice calling from the other side of the bluff. "Over here!" he yelled back. "We're just over the rocks."

Minutes later, their father half-rolled, half-fell down the steep face. "Dad!" David forgot why he'd run away. He forgot to be angry. He ran to his father and threw his arms around him. "I didn't expect to see you."

"That's my fault," his dad replied.

"Daddy! David?" Laura struggled to sit up. "I hear Daddy!"

"Laura's hurt." David rushed back to his sister. "You're not imagining things," he said. "Dad's here. We're going to be okay."

"I'm right here, Laura." Their father knelt down and touched her hot forehead. He turned worried eyes on David. "What happened?"

"Laura fell," David said shortly. "My fault. Her leg … I guess I really blew it."

Their dad lifted the edge of the sleeping bag off Laura's fractured leg and examined it closely. "You're a brave girl," he said, ashen-faced. "Are you in a lot of pain?"

"Not so bad now," she murmured. "David made a fire so we'd be rescued."

"You did the right thing, David. The splint is brilliant. The Coast Guard is on its way. Paul and Jennifer are waiting where you left the dinghy to direct them."

In the distance, they heard the rumble of a powerful engine. Soon the running lights of a vessel appeared out of the darkness, heading directly toward them. David eyed it carefully. "That's not the Coast Guard. That's Drifter McGee! He's going to kill us for taking his boat!"

Drifter hove to and anchored his boat in the shallow waters. "Did you kids steal my boat?" he yelled over the breaking waves.

David's father elbowed him gently. "Go ahead, answer him."

"Yes, sir."

"Did you wreck it?"

"No, sir."

"Good. Are you okay?"

"No!" David shouted. "Laura's leg's broken!"

"I'll radio Coast Guard." Drifter disappeared inside the cabin of his trawler. He reappeared a minute later. "They'll send in a bird!" he called. "Where's my goddamn boat?"

"Radio Paul!" David's father yelled back. "He's keeping your boat safe. Tell him we'll see him back on Fern."

Drifter grunted in their general direction, lifted his anchor and extinguished the search light, heading off to claim his dinghy.

David grinned. He'd learned a thing or two about Drifter. He wasn't crazy — and he had a big heart.

While their father sat beside Laura, David added wood to the fire. "It'll help them see us."

Half an hour later, they heard the whirring sound of a helicopter. Laura's eyes fluttered open. "Daddy?"

"It's all right, honey. It's the chopper."

"Daddy! I need to ask you something."

"Shoot."

"David and I heard everything. We don't want to go back to Toronto. Not yet. Do we have to?"

Silence. The waves tiptoed across the sand almost noiselessly.

Finally, after what seemed a long time, their father spoke. "I made a mistake." He spoke haltingly. "I promise you that from now on things are going to be different. Your aunt and I have talked. We've got a plan. I can't say a lot more, but I promise you that not everything you overheard was the truth."

"Where's Kathleen?" David asked.

"Phil O'Reilly took her to Powell River to catch a flight out — but Kathleen's not the problem, David."

"I just asked."

David's father looked tired, deep lines criss-crossing his brow. "David," he said, "and Laura. I'm so sorry about all of this. I love you. Both of you."

Laura smiled and took his hand. "I love you, too, Daddy."

David began to kick sand onto the fire. "Yeah, me too," he said, his eyes fixed on the dying flames.

When the Coast Guard helicopter, guided by a skilled pilot and a powerful light, landed on the uneven beach, they had to shield their faces from the blowing sand. Two paramedics exited and rushed to Laura. They examined her quickly but thoroughly, administered morphine, re-splinted her leg and loaded her into the helicopter. David and his father climbed in behind her. David's ride was brief. The Coast Guard dropped him off on Fern Island, then continued with Laura and her father to the trauma unit at St. Paul's Hospital in Vancouver, as her injury was too serious to be treated locally.

Aunt Jenn stood on the beach, but it was Drifter, who'd arrived almost simultaneously, that David wanted to see first. He approached the old man cautiously.

"Didn't anyone teach you how to tie up a boat properly?" he snapped at David. "You could have lost my dinghy!"

"I'm sorry, but you got it back, didn't you?"

"Good thing, too." He cleared his throat and spat. "I reckon you almost owed me a boat. Little thief! How's the girl?"

David smiled. "She'll be all right. In a cast for a while, but she should be okay. Thanks to everyone who went looking for us. You, too," he added softly. "I owe you."

Drifter grunted and looked away.

"One more thing," said David. "We saw you the other day, out on the water with the whale watchers. You did a good thing."

"Bloody fools!" Drifter spat again.

"We could help you," David offered, getting the words out quickly. "Aunt Jennifer says only some of them are the problem. A few bad apples spoil the barrel. We could get a meeting together … figure out a way to make sure the rules are enforced … it's being done in other places."

Drifter shuffled away, then turned back to David. "I ain't goin' to no meetings," he growled, "but I'm taking your word that you and your aunt will. That way, I forgive you for the thieving of my boat."

David grinned widely. "You've got yourself a deal." He stuck out his hand and shook Drifter's solidly. The old man's callused palm gripped his.

"Good," said Drifter. "I'll hold you to it."

Chapter Fifteen

AUNT Jennifer waited impatiently for David to finish his conversation with Drifter before throwing her arms around her nephew. "I'll make an enormous feast — all your favourite things, David. Drifter, you'll have to return for dinner." She turned to Matthew, who'd joined the crowd on the wharf. "You too, of course. Tonight will be a celebration."

Drifter shook his head gruffly, and motioned to Aunt Jennifer to untie his mooring lines. "I'm not one for socializing, haven't been, least not since God was a boy, but thanks for the offer."

He disappeared into the cabin and the engines on his big boat hummed to life. He reappeared on the deck and addressed Aunt Jennifer. "Your boy made me a promise. I'll be holding him to it. Shove me off."

Aunt Jennifer smiled and pushed the *Corky*'s heavy bow out toward the sea. "Thanks, Drifter!" she called. "For everything."

Drifter tipped his hat in their general direction. The big trawler headed off toward Sand Dollar Bay. David and Aunt Jennifer watched until she'd disappeared around the point, then they linked arms and walked slowly up the ramp, down the long pier and on through the woods to the cabin. On the way, David told Aunt Jennifer everything. She listened quietly, occasionally nodding her head in approval, wincing at the description of Laura's fall. She didn't speak until David had finished, then she said, "Good things will come out of this."

"It was a terrible risk," David said. "I know that now. Laura …"

"Laura should be fine. I'll bet she'll be back on Fern Island by the weekend." Aunt Jennifer dug into her pocket and offered David a cold Coke, which he accepted gratefully. "In the meantime, your dad and I have come up with a solution that will work for everyone, including your mother." She held up her hand. "Don't ask. It'll be better if we speak to you and your sister together." She put her arm around David's shoulder and squeezed. "Sometimes we have to take a risk to make people see things. I support what you did, David."

"Mum? Is she … does she?"

"Your mother is no better or worse than she was a few days ago. Her moods have stabilized — but David, she'll be on medication. It's the only way she'll cope successfully. The doctors feel very positive that along with counselling, she'll function quite well in the world."

"Sounds bleak," David replied. "I don't want to live like that anymore."

"David, you have to trust me. Wait until your sister returns. Things are going to work out. You'll see."

Oddly enough, David did trust her. She'd never given him any reason not to. He cleaned himself up, devoured a double helping of bacon and eggs, then climbed into bed. He slept most of the day — a sleep devoid of guilt or fear. By the time he and his aunt sat down at the table with Matthew and his family — a table loaded with poached salmon, roasted potatoes, sour cream, blackberry-apple pie and fresh blueberries — he felt positively happy. They ate until they were bursting and then they ate more. After dinner, at Aunt Jennifer's suggestion, the boys ran to Matthew's to fetch his overnight gear. That night the boys sat up talking, laughing and counting shooting stars, until Aunt Jennifer shooed them off to bed still full and content.

David's father stayed at Laura's bedside in Vancouver until the following Friday, returning to the island with her on Paul's regularly scheduled afternoon flight. Paul dropped off the Fern Island passengers last, and announced to everyone's joy that he would be spending the night.

Everyone made a fuss over Laura's cast, which went from her ankle to her thigh. "Sign it, David," she begged, brandishing a pink marker.

His father had written: *To my favourite and bravest girl, love Daddy.* Paul wrote: *To my favourite cast-a-way!* David scrawled in big letters: DRAGON ISLAND, SHARK'S TOOTH, DESOLATION SOUND!

Aunt Jennifer wrote: *Next time you run away, let me know and I'll join you!* David and Laura laughed, because they knew she meant it. Their father promised to transport Laura in her wheelbarrow chariot down to Matthew and Christine's later on for more autographs. "But first," he said, "it's time for a family conference."

Aunt Jennifer settled Laura on a chaise longue, under the leafy branches of the arbutus tree, and the others sat around the table where Aunt Jennifer had set a large pitcher of fresh lemonade.

Paul accepted a glass, then stood up and glanced warmly at Aunt Jennifer. "I'll go for a walk, then." He bent to kiss her.

"Paul, please stay." She took his arm in hers and smiled shyly at her family. "Paul and I ..." she hesitated. David had never seen his aunt at a loss for words. "We've talked ... well, how would you kids like to have a pilot for an uncle?"

Laura squealed in delight. David cheered and their father thumped Paul on the back before planting a large kiss on Aunt

Jennifer's red cheek. "This is good news," said their father. "Elizabeth will be thrilled."

"Elizabeth always thought I should marry," agreed Aunt Jennifer. "But the right guy never asked me …" she squeezed Paul's hand, "until now."

Elizabeth. His mother. The piece of the puzzle that didn't fit … Her name propelled David into his own uncertain future. His face crumpled and he glanced sideways at his sister. Her singular concentration on her cast and her refusal to meet his eyes confirmed that she felt the same worry he did. She twirled a strand of hair around her finger.

The adults, oblivious, continued talking. "Elizabeth will be pleased," Aunt Jennifer said. "But we're jumping ahead. I just didn't want Paul to feel he has to rush off." She looked at him fondly. "After all, he'll soon be part of the family."

Paul sat, clearly pleased to be included. He nodded at David and Laura's father. "Go ahead."

"When we discovered you and Laura gone," their father began, "I felt sick at heart, and angry, too." He worried an arbutus leaf, rolling and unrolling it in the palm of his hand as he spoke. "The anger, I realized, was directed not at you two, but at myself. Your aunt helped me to see a lot of things that morning."

"We quickly realized you and Laura must have overheard us talking out here the night before," Aunt Jennifer interjected. "Why else would you run away? We were all terrified you'd do something dangerous. We knew you'd heard your dad and I talking about the family history … about genes and depression and so forth."

David thought about the choppy sea and Drifter's dinghy pitching and rolling through the narrow channel. He smelled the cold, salty air and heard Laura's scream. He shuddered.

"We knew you might believe your future was bleak, so why worry about your present?" his father added.

David nodded imperceptibly. He'd felt that way. Exactly that way. Still did.

"But you see …" as Aunt Jennifer struggled to find the right words, Paul covered her hand with one of his own. "But you see, I owe you an apology. Nobody knew the truth. Not your father, not you and not even your mother. Lies upon lies."

David shifted forward in his chair. Laura stopped twirling her hair and looked up.

"Lies?" David's eyes jumped between his aunt and his father. "I don't understand."

"Of course not. Let me explain." Aunt Jennifer sighed deeply. "When my mother, your grandmother, was a young woman in the late 1940s, she, well, she fell in love with a man the family didn't approve of. They refused to grant her permission to marry the man she loved, and in their social circle one didn't marry without permission. My mother was a stubborn woman. She didn't marry him, but they had two children together — your mother and me. It caused a terrible scandal. A scandal the family tried to cover up forever."

"I don't understand."

"Just listen, Laura," said David. "What happened?"

"Your great-grandparents made their lives miserable, so miserable in fact, that my real father left when I was only two and your mother was a baby. They paid him off, gave him a great deal of money to disappear. It broke your grandmother's heart. She was never the same again. Depressed? Yes, but who wouldn't be? Her parents arranged a marriage to the man you knew from photos as your grandfather. *He* committed suicide when you were both very young. *He* was very disturbed, but he wasn't related to your mother."

"You mean," David said, piecing it all together, "he wasn't really your dad or our grandfather. He didn't die of a heart attack, but his genes weren't Mum's genes."

"Exactly."

"So Laura and I don't come from a family plagued by generations of depression?"

"No. No, you don't, but even if you did, it doesn't mean anything. You are in control of your own fate," Aunt Jennifer continued. "But just so you know, my real father, the one who disappeared, had a perfectly healthy family history. Still, no one ever talked about him and I had no memory of him. I guess I never really thought much about it until your mum became ill. It became a family secret, hidden, I'm ashamed to say, even from your mother. I only told your father after we discovered you and Laura had run away."

"But you knew. You knew the whole time," David said.

"I found out going through my own mother's diaries after she'd died fifteen years ago. I never breathed a word to anyone until I spoke to your father the other morning. Things were different in those days … At least, I don't know, I don't have an excuse for what I've done, and it never occurred to me that your mother or the rest of you might think she'd inherited a genetic tendency to mental illness."

"And all those years, your parents and all your relatives went along with the story?" Paul did not try to hide his incredulity.

"They just never talked about it. When Mother died, I didn't see any point in changing the story. I was wrong." Aunt Jennifer looked sheepishly at David and Laura.

"Do you mean," David asserted, still not quite sure he understood, "that there is no genetic illness in our family? So Laura and I will be okay and Mum's depression is all in her head, not real at all?"

"No, there is no genetic mental illness in our family. Yes, you and Laura will be fine. And no, to your final question." Aunt Jennifer struggled to make herself understood. "Your mother has a severe depression. It probably began years ago, but none of us really paid much attention. Sometimes she could be moody, or sad, but can't we all? But it was more than that with your mother, and none of us knew how to read the signs. It's not genetic, but that's beside the point. It doesn't matter. What matters is that she needs professional help and her family's support. You kids have helped her more than you ever should have had to. Now it's up to your dad and me."

"Dad and you," David repeated. He turned to his father, but didn't dare speak the words in his mind.

Laura did. "Does that mean you and Mum are getting back together?" she asked hopefully.

"No. No, honey. At least I haven't closed any doors, but I don't think so. I hope that even if you can't understand that, you can respect it. It means I'm going to do everything I can to make the best of this situation, for all of us, but especially for you and David and your mother."

"No fairytale endings," David mumbled. He reached into his pocket and felt the smooth gold band he'd taken off the table just a few nights ago. It seemed like a lifetime away. He'd return it to his father, he decided. It didn't belong with him. It belonged in a world unfamiliar to him, a place his parents inhabited, a place he no longer felt responsible for.

"However," his father ignored the interruption, "I've spoken at great length with your mother, and your aunt and Kathleen. I'd like to run an idea by you two now. What would you think about moving out to the West Coast? There's a company in

Vancouver that's willing to hire me and your aunt … Actually …" he turned to Aunt Jennifer. "Why don't you go ahead? You planted the seed."

Aunt Jennifer couldn't sit still in her excitement. She stood up and paced back and forth in front of them. "We've all decided that if you kids agree, the best place, the most healing place for your mother is right here on Fern Island. It's close to Vancouver so she can go in for counselling, and you two could spend all your holidays and every second weekend with us." She smiled at Paul. "I know a great pilot who'd be happy to ferry you back and forth!"

Laura didn't hesitate. "Yippee!" she cried. "We get to stay! Mum will get better in Bliss Cove and I don't have to go back to David's disgusting cooking!"

David didn't dare look at anyone. He was afraid to break the spell, afraid to find out it was all just another adult lie. He spoke carefully, pronouncing each syllable clearly and choosing each word deliberately. "So, what you guys are saying is that Laura, Dad and I can live in Vancouver, we'd go to school there. Mum will live in Bliss Cove and sometimes in the city. She might get better and she might not, but she'd be happier, and I wouldn't have to … I wouldn't have to look after her."

Aunt Jennifer smiled across the table at David. His father stood up and walked over to his son. He knelt down until they were at eye level. Still David had difficulty looking directly at him. "David," he said. "That's exactly what we're saying. That is, if it works for you. You should never have had to run away for us to come to our senses, but now that you're safely back, I'm glad you did."

"Thanks, Dad," David said simply. "But what about Kathleen?"

"Kathleen will have a lot to think about — her job is a big one. I guess we'll have to wait and see what happens. It's not something you have to worry about. Give the worrying back to me."

David looked into his father's eyes and smiled. "Okay. It works for us."

Laura suddenly exclaimed, "Hey, if we're going to live in Vancouver, can we learn to ski?" She looked down at her cast. "I mean, after my leg's better ..."

They all laughed. "I guess you're still the risk-taker," said David.

"I'd say you both are!" Aunt Jennifer retorted, grinning. "Now, if everything's settled, let's eat dinner. I've made lasagna, Caesar salad, garlicky cheese bread, plus an apple pie, a blueberry pie and chocolate chip cookies."

They all groaned. "I'm going to have to double my exercise routine," Paul laughed. But they all managed to eat a large dinner, then inhale a slice of fresh pie and a handful of cookies.

After dinner, Paul and David sauntered down to the wharf together to check on the Beaver. Paul said casually, "If you know of anyone who'd like a ride in an airplane, I'd be happy to oblige." He winked at David, then bent down and began untying the mooring lines.

Ten minutes later, high in the air over Desolation Sound, David gazed down at the wilderness that in a few short weeks he'd come to love, and that now he could begin to think of as home.

"What about Kathleen, though?" he asked Paul. "What if she ends up moving out here?"

"You worry too much, kid!" he boomed through the headphones. "Some things are better left to time. My motto is *carpe diem*."

"*Carpe diem*?" repeated David.

Paul brought the Beaver around in a loose circle and dipped down toward Bliss Cove. The sunlight reflecting off the ocean shimmered and danced below them like liquid diamonds. Out in the strait, a spray of water shot out of the sea, and David knew there were whales nearby.

Paul nodded. "*Carpe diem*. Enjoy the moment!"

Acknowledgements

MANY thanks to all those who supported me through the process of writing this book. In particular, I'd like to acknowledge Phil Mundy and Rebecca Fairbairn for the time they dedicated to reading the early drafts, and for their encouraging and insightful comments.

I'd also like to thank Joy Gugeler for believing that this was a story that needed to be told and Elizabeth McLean for the meticulous and astute editing she demonstrated throughout the process of developing this book.

Orcalab2001 provided valuable information on killer whales and I recommend a visit to their website at <www.orcalab.org> for anyone who is interested in observing and studying these magnificent marine mammals in their natural habitat.

Much appreciation to Jonathan Stewart for sharing with me his extensive knowledge of boats, engines, tides, winds and other things nautical.

Finally, I'd like to thank my family for graciously accepting that sometimes the creative process takes precedence over everything else.

Note to the Reader

ONE in four people suffers from depression or a related anxiety disorder. It is nothing to be ashamed of, but it is destructive to both people suffering from depression and their loved ones. Support groups are available to help. If you or somebody in your family is experiencing the following symptoms:

- extended bouts of sadness or irritation
- lethargy
- appetite change (either loss of appetite or compulsive eating)
- loss of interest or obsessive interest in hobbies
- loss of enjoyment of time spent with family or friends
- trouble concentrating
- disturbed sleep patterns
- feeling tired all the time
- no energy
- feelings of guilt or worthlessness
- extremely low self-esteem
- sense of hopelessness
- thoughts or actions of self-hurt
- thoughts of suicide

CALL YOUR FAMILY DOCTOR. Most forms of depression are treatable.

About the Author

ADRIFT is Julie Burtinshaw's second Young Adult novel. She lives in Vancouver with her family.

PHOTO: PETER MOFFAT

Other Raincoast Fiction
for Young Adults and Teens:

Dead Reckoning by Julie Burtinshaw
1-55192-342-4 $9.95 CDN • $6.95 US

The Outside Chance of Maximilian Glick by Morley Torgov
1-55192-548-6 $12.95 CDN

Stickler and Me by Morley Torgov
1-555192-546-X $12.95 CDN

Spitfire by Ann Goldring
1-55192-490-0 $9.95 CDN • $6.95 US

My Brother's Keeper by Marion Woodson
1-55192-488-9 $9.95 CDN • $6.95 US

Wishing Star Summer by Beryl Young
1-55192-450-1 $9.95 CDN • $6.95 US

The Accomplice by Norma Charles
1-55192-430-7 $9.95 CDN • $6.95 US

Cat's Eye Corner by Terry Griggs
1-55192-350-5 $9.95 CDN • $6.95 US

Raven's Flight by Diane Silvey
1-55192-344-0 $9.95 CDN • $6.95 US